one foot wrong.

one foot wrong.

a novel.   sofie laguna.

other press. new york.

Other Press edition 2009

First published in 2008 by Allen & Unwin, Crows Nest, New South
Wales, Australia

Production Editor: Yvonne E. Cárdenas
Book design: Simon M. Sullivan

This book was set in 11.5 pt Caslon by Alpha Design & Composition
of Pittsfield, NH.

10 9 8 7 6 5 4 3 2 1

Quotes from "Lord of the Dance" by Sydney B. Carter and "Morning
Has Broken" by Eleanor Farjeon reproduced with permission.

LIBRARY OF CONGRESS CATALOGING-IN-PUBLICATION DATA
Laguna, Sofie, 1968–
One foot wrong : a novel / Sofie Laguna.
p. cm.
ISBN 978-1-59051-316-3 (acid-free paper)—ISBN 978-1-59051-
334-7 (e-book) 1. Imaginary companions—Fiction. 2. Child abuse—
Religious aspects—Fiction. 3. Psychological fiction. I. Title.
PR9619.4.L34064 2009
823'.92—dc22   2009000943

PUBLISHER'S NOTE:
This is a work of fiction. Names, characters, places, and incidents either
are the product of the author's imagination or are used fictitiously, and
any resemblance to actual persons, living or dead, events, or locales is
entirely coincidental.

There is a lion in the way; a lion is in the streets.

Proverbs 26:13

one foot wrong.

I slept at the feet of Boot and Sack. My one small bed went longways across the end of their big one. If I turned my head in the night and the moon was shining through, I could see the hill of Boot's feet beside my face. Sack's feet I couldn't see but I knew they were there—no shoes, tipped over, and sleeping.

Every night Sack pulled my blankets tight around me, pressing me down. "Lie still, Hester, not a peep from you, not a wriggle." Every night I lay on my back looking up through the dark at the gray paint cloud, at its cracks in the shapes of wings, and the white curtain sometimes blowing.

Cat was there and together we'd wait for the bird dream. Cat's bird dream was hiding in the long grass, a fast chase, and a jump. In my bird dream everything was white without walls. Bird sang and flew and so did I. Then bird became many birds. Every part of me moved with the many birds—my fingers, hair, and toes all swirled and twirled in bird circles. Which was me and which was bird?

A secret has no sound; it lives in your darkest corner, where it sits and waits. Sometimes it gives a jump or a wriggle but mostly it waits like the spider waits for the fly. A secret grows thick like the ball of web the spider weaves around the fly when he makes the trap. Fly can't breathe or smell in there—his world sticks against his face, small as his own eyes.

I sat on the floor with Cat. Cat rolled on her back, then jumped for the yellow wool. I pulled it from her and she jumped again. She twisted her body in the air and spun herself around. She ran under the table, then ran back to me. Sack was sewing, her foot pumping the floor *pump pump pump*, the needle sticking the white cloth *stick stick stick*. A tickle grew in me.

Yellow wool wrapped itself around Cat's black paws; she rolled onto her back, wool curled around her tum. It went around and around her until Cat was in a yellow tangle. Every way she moved she tangled more. Cat was playing like the children at Christ's feet when he made a visit to the marketplace in *The Abridged Picture Bible*.

The tickle in me grew bigger; it pushed at my nose and mouth wanting to escape. Cat jumped and twisted and fell against me. My mouth was shut tight; I was holding that tickling laugh back because I knew it was trouble. Cat jumped on my lap and then that laugh burst out of me, like a sneeze from my toes up.

I laughed at black Cat turning and turning, her shining black-gray body caught in the net of yellow wool. I laughed and laughed. I couldn't stop. What went in through my eyes tickled the inside of me and made me laugh louder. I was shaking with it. Sack was up and out of her sewing seat, scissors fell from her knee, she held my chin in her hard sewing fingers, and she shook my face from one side to the other, her two blue eyes looking into mine.

"You laugh like the devil. I swear there's a devil in you!" The laugh went out of me and wriggled its way into her fingers that were holding my chin. I couldn't hear it anymore after that; it was hidden somewhere inside Sack. Laughing was the same as crying; it left you empty as air.

A devil in me . . . Is his home in the bone down my back? Does the devil live in the same place in me that the laugh comes from? Somewhere down deep, a place you can't touch with a finger?

Sack said, "When you're bigger you can move into the empty room where you will be by yourself."

"When will that be?" I asked her.

"When I say," she said. I walked into the empty room that would be mine when Sack said, and I sat on the floor. Cat was there too. The room wasn't empty anymore—it had Hester in it, and Cat. I wondered how many times the hands would go around the face of the kitchen clock above the stove before Sack said.

Boot found me sitting there. "You know this is not allowed!"

Sack heard him and came running up the stairs hissing like Cat in a corner. "Don't you push me, young lady, don't you do it!" She slapped my ear. It put a ringing bell in my head; the more I listened the louder it got until it was a whole song with words and the bell to go with it. Not a song from Sack's radio box, not a song that Sack ever heard. It made me smile; it was a secret song just for me.

I sat and I sat and I ate what was put before me. Chicken legs, oats and milk, pork and corn, bread and oil. The chicken legs used to be a walking chicken. "Why did it stop walking?" I asked Boot when he was carving. Sack hadn't come back from folding sheets in the laundry.

Boot patted my head. "Unlucky," he said. The oil made the bread heavy. I pushed it with my sharp fork.

Sack came back. "Don't play with your food, Hester, eat it. John, the fire needs wood." Boot left the kitchen. I put the bread in my mouth but I couldn't chew. Teeth and tongue said no. The heavy bread filled every space. I couldn't swallow. Sack was watching, waiting for the bread to go down into the deep of Hester, but it wouldn't. It stuck.

"Eat it." There wasn't anywhere else to look but Sack's face. The bread took up all the other room. "What are you doing, Hester? I told you to eat your dinner." Sack had two blue eyes with a pink stain under—one the shape of a small spider with three legs. The pink spider glowed pinker as Sack watched me with the stuck angry bread. Suddenly her hand was at my mouth and she was digging and pushing at the bread. "Greedy, *greedy*, you took so much from me!" Her fingers clawed at the insides of my cheeks like Cat clawed at the carpet.

Sack pushed down the angry bread with her fingers. I couldn't get the air past the bread and fingers. The angry bread filled the room with its shouting *no no no!* Boot came running back into the kitchen. He pulled Sack off and held her by her shoulders. The pink spider turned in tiny circles under her eye. Sack was shaking. Boot told her to have a lie-down upstairs. He gave me water. I drank the water. "I'm afraid you'll have to stay there until you've eaten it all up," Boot said. I tasted blood.

I lay on the hallway floor and ran my fingers down the dark cracks between the boards. Sack was in the laundry telling Boot he did it wrong. I couldn't hear the words of Boot's answer, only his soft sound. He wanted Sack to be quiet. Sack's voice was a thin line; Boot's was wet as a bucket of leak-water.

The tickle in me grew bigger; it pushed at my nose and mouth wanting to escape. Cat jumped and twisted and fell against me. My mouth was shut tight; I was holding that tickling laugh back because I knew it was trouble. Cat jumped on my lap and then that laugh burst out of me, like a sneeze from my toes up.

I laughed at black Cat turning and turning, her shining black-gray body caught in the net of yellow wool. I laughed and laughed. I couldn't stop. What went in through my eyes tickled the inside of me and made me laugh louder. I was shaking with it. Sack was up and out of her sewing seat, scissors fell from her knee, she held my chin in her hard sewing fingers, and she shook my face from one side to the other, her two blue eyes looking into mine.

"You laugh like the devil. I swear there's a devil in you!" The laugh went out of me and wriggled its way into her fingers that were holding my chin. I couldn't hear it anymore after that; it was hidden somewhere inside Sack. Laughing was the same as crying; it left you empty as air.

A devil in me . . . Is his home in the bone down my back? Does the devil live in the same place in me that the laugh comes from? Somewhere down deep, a place you can't touch with a finger?

Sack said, "When you're bigger you can move into the empty room where you will be by yourself."

"When will that be?" I asked her.

"When I say," she said. I walked into the empty room that would be mine when Sack said, and I sat on the floor. Cat was there too. The room wasn't empty anymore—it had Hester in it, and Cat. I wondered how many times the hands would go around the face of the kitchen clock above the stove before Sack said.

Boot found me sitting there. "You know this is not allowed!"

Sack heard him and came running up the stairs hissing like Cat in a corner. "Don't you push me, young lady, don't you do it!" She slapped my ear. It put a ringing bell in my head; the more I listened the louder it got until it was a whole song with words and the bell to go with it. Not a song from Sack's radio box, not a song that Sack ever heard. It made me smile; it was a secret song just for me.

I sat and I sat and I ate what was put before me. Chicken legs, oats and milk, pork and corn, bread and oil. The chicken legs used to be a walking chicken. "Why did it stop walking?" I asked Boot when he was carving. Sack hadn't come back from folding sheets in the laundry.

Boot patted my head. "Unlucky," he said. The oil made the bread heavy. I pushed it with my sharp fork.

Sack came back. "Don't play with your food, Hester, eat it. John, the fire needs wood." Boot left the kitchen. I put the bread in my mouth but I couldn't chew. Teeth and tongue said no. The heavy bread filled every space. I couldn't swallow. Sack was watching, waiting for the bread

"Turn me, Hester," handle said. I stepped closer. "I am your friend, turn me."

"What is a friend?" I asked him.

"A friend gives you pictures," he said. I reached out and turned him. The back door swung open and I stepped out. I was looking at the forbidden world with a tree in it.

I stepped down into the long green grass. It scratched my legs where my socks finished. The tree was a different tree than the one in Jesus's paradise. This one had no leaves and it went every way just like the flames from the fire in the red wood stove. It was as if the flames had stopped moving and become tree. Tree reached up like Hester reaching for the handle. She reached up with all her many flame fingers. I looked to where she reached, *up up* into the sky. What handle did tree want to turn? What door did tree want to open?

The sun burned hot in my face. The sky was the home of the sun. The sun was there when Jesus rose on the fifth day in his white dress. Two ladies saw when they walked past on their way to the shop. Jesus wanted to go to the same place as tree. Tree wanted to open the door to the home of the sun! I stood and looked until drips came from my burning eyes.

I walked to the other side; socks without feet inside and trousers empty of legs hung from the line. Boot's shirts hung upside down by their arms. No hands, body, or neck of Boot inside. Boot's hands, body, and neck were in the kitchen being shouted at by Sack. I could still hear the black line of her words. "You didn't look, you never used your eyes!" The shirts waved their empty arms in the wind.

I walked down through the scratching grass to tree. I touched her trunk and pressed my ear close. "Hester . . . pretty . . . beautiful Hester . . ." Those were the words from the wood of tree; she sent them straight down the tunnels of my ears and into the place where messages came. I put my lips to her thick body and kissed like Sack kissed Cat's head, *kiss kiss*.

The tree was full of little lines making shapes and bumps, like somebody drew into tree with Sack's sharp list-pencil. I saw pictures of mice and a bottle and a wing. Who had been living out here drawing secret pictures into the body of tree? Was it *a friend*?

I bent down so my knees came up close to my face and I patted the ground around tree. A line of ants moved across the stony ground, one following the other. I put my finger in the line and the ants climbed over. A finger couldn't stop them. I lay on my tum with my face close to the moving line. I watched the ants quickly walking. I rolled over to look behind me. Would a line of Hesters be following? I watched the ants walk into a small dark hole. They followed each other down. Were they going home? What was down there? How did the ants know it was their home?

I looked at the stony dirt. Stones all shapes; every one different. I could have made a crown of stones with string, and butter for glue. I could have put it on my head and done a prayer in a circle dance. I picked up two stones; I rolled them around in my hands. I felt the edges. Who made them? Who did they belong to?

I looked into the grass. I saw flowers. They were smaller than the ones in the Garden of Eden and there were more of them. The pink flowers were like tiny colored hats in the grass. The orange flowers wore skirts and in the middle of the orange skirt was the seeing eye. Through the seeing eye the flower saw the way dirt moves, each piece up against another, always changing places. The orange flowers wore skirts for the dance of feet passing. The purple flowers were teacups full of tea that tasted like honey. I put my face up close and took a small sip. I closed my eyes. Blankets of purple, orange, and pink came down over me.

I lay and listened to the sound of ants walking. I listened to the pencil making pictures in tree and I listened to tree reaching for the handle to the door of the home of the sun.

I heard another sound too, deep inside, in a part you couldn't put a finger on. It was Sack shouting at Boot for all she was worth. Soon she would go looking for me in the bedroom where I should have been, on the floor reading *The Abridged Picture Bible*. Then there'd be trouble. Sack would be shouting for all she worth at *me* then. I stood up and ran through the grass back to the steps and the door. I turned and I looked at the forbidden outside—no window with dust between me and the world—one last time. I was Lot's wife on the cliff looking back. Would the outside go away when I closed the door? I looked until I could see it with my eyes shut, then walked through the door and closed it behind me.

I was shut inside the house now. The walls and the ceiling and the floor told me when to stop, the way the spider's web tells the fly when to stop. Somewhere there were Boot and Sack but I didn't know where. One Cott Road was quiet, though Sack's words still bounced around the room: *John, times, God, why on earth?, disappoint, you.* The only thing missing was her mouth with the dark tunnel leading down to where her messages came. I crept like Cat, past the words as they knocked against the walls and floor, looking for an ear to reach. I climbed the stairs *one step two step three step four*, past the room that would be mine when Sack said, until I got to the master bedroom. I took *The Abridged Picture Bible* out from under my bed, opened it, and touched Lot's wife with my fingers. She stood on the high cliff with her face turned back, the color of ash. Her coat flew out behind like a hard wing. She was looking for the line of Lot's wives. They weren't there and that made Lot's wife sad. "Lot," I said, "Lot, where are you? Have you eaten your dinner, Lot? You better eat it all up."

"Hester, I'm coming in a moment to check on you," Sack called from the toilet. I heard it flush. I turned the page so Lot's wife could go to sleep, and I waited for Sack to come and check on me.

It was night and I could hear the sleep-breathing of Boot and Sack *in out in out in out*. Boot breathed as if the air was heavy as a bag of flour. Sack only breathed on the way out. A small whistle. Every night my song sang itself to the tune of their breathing. I turned on my back and pulled my arms out from under the tight covers. I closed my eyes and I saw the tree from outside. She was reaching up and then I reached up too, spreading my flame fingers as far as they could go—far enough to split—*up up up* to the home of the sun.

"I wish you wouldn't," Sack said to Boot when he tasted the soup that sat on the stove. When she was gone for a lie-down I asked him, "What is a wish?" He turned to me, soup caught in the hairs under his mouth. "Why won't you call me *daddy*, or *papa*, or *father?*"

"What is a wish?" I asked again.

"What is a *what?*"

"What is a wish?"

He looked down at me, then up again and into the faraway. "It is something you want very much."

"Why can't you have it?"

"Different reasons. Something stops you." I made my back hard and straight. *Something you want very much . . .* I wanted a pencil.

Cat was one of the Lord's creeping creatures. She slept on a thin pillow by the step. Sack fed her, Boot fed her, and I did too. Cat was gray and black with a bit missing from her ear and a tail with a bend. I always knew where she was and she always knew where I was. She never came when I wanted to touch her head and look at where her missing bit was. She hissed at me when I put my face close. Sometimes Cat and me ate together, both of us under the table. Sack said, "Until you learn, you are no more than a dirty thing on all fours." I looked into Cat's eyes while we shared the bones.

Cat caught mice. She brought them inside, put them between her paws, and knocked them on the head. They tried to run away but they couldn't run fast enough with blood out the nose and a torn ear. Cat let them get a little way, just far enough to think they could get home to the hole in the wall, and then she knocked them on the head again. The mice tried to walk but it was getting harder with blood on the side and an eye out. I lay on the floor and watched. Soon the mice couldn't walk at all. They lay still and quiet and that's when Cat walked away.

Cat had climbed up on the mantelpiece and was playing with the list-pencil that Sack hung from the wall by a piece of string. Cat knocked it one way, then another, with her black paw. I sat under the chair and watched. She kept pulling. The pencil was coming loose from the string. Soon Cat knocked the list-pencil so hard it dropped to the floor. I jumped out from under the table, picked it up, and hid it in my pants.

Different reasons weren't stopping me from having my wish anymore.

I went to the shelf of books. I reached back into the row behind the row, and I took a book from the very end. Nobody had touched the book for a long time. It had dust along the top. On the cover of the book was a king on a throne. Lot's wife was the queen standing beside him. Her hand was on his shoulder and she was smiling. She held a long stick and wore a crown of pointed stones. The stones were stuck together with butter from the cooling cupboard. Every page of the book was covered in little black marks with space around the sides as if the line of ants had walked in twisting circle paths, and then somebody closed the book with a snap and squashed them flat. Boot asked, *Should we teach her to read?* and Sack said, *She doesn't have the wherewithal. Wherewithal* is what you need to read and go outside. I don't have it because I came late to my mother. She nearly lost her life to the birth of me. *All those years of waiting and longing, and for what? For this?*

I flicked through the pages of the book. Dust fell off the paper, and the pages were brown at the corners. The book needed a friend. I hid it in my pants with the pencil, then walked up the stairs to the bedroom. Sack was out on a visit. Boot was in his study listening to the radio. I was locked inside with my wish. It was hard walking up the stairs with a book and a pencil hidden in my pants but I could do it. I was the Lord's mistake but I could do it.

I went into the bedroom and crawled under the bed with my head out the side for light. I took the book and the pencil from my pants. I opened the book and found a page without so many squashed ant marks. I put the pencil to the paper the way Sack did when she wrote a list. A list was a line of things that Sack wanted Boot to bring home from the shop. *We will need flour, and tea. And don't forget soap.* I wrote my own list in secret writing. On my list I put *outside*, I put *a skirt*, I put *a crown of stones.* I tried to make my writing look like the words in the book but soon the pencil didn't want to write a list. It wanted to do other things. I watched my hand move across the paper. The pencil made the shape of the tree; the marks that were already there on the page became leaves and a nest. Then it made the shape of God the Bird flying through the branches of the tree. He had a sheep with him; the sheep had a wing. If my pencil was green the sheep would be too. My pencil made the home of the sun. It had circle doors but it didn't have walls or a floor. Through the circle doors you could see gardens full with orange and purple flowers. The gardens floated in the sky. Then my pencil made the pink spider under Sack's eye, then it drew her eye, and then it drew the soup caught in the hairs under Boot's mouth, then the hairs turned into water, then it made Lot's wife but this time she was moving, she was flying from the cliff out over the gray seas, her coat spread like the wings of a bird, and then it made the seas parting, fish flew out, and then it ran out of pencil. The pencil was flat. I pushed the flat pencil harder into the page of the book and it made a small hole.

There is no need to cry. You are not a baby anymore. I crawled further back under the bed and I put the pencil where the carpet meets the wall. The flat pencil was my secret. I put the book back in my pants and I crawled out from under the bed. I walked downstairs—Sack was not back from her visit—and

I went to the shelf. I put the book back onto the very end of the row behind the row.

I was stirring the stew when someone spoke to me. Sack was in the living room tapping her foot to *Alleluia* coming from the radio box. Boot was outside chopping wood. It was the wooden spoon in my hand who had spoken to me. It was only a whisper and hard to hear. I had to bend close to the stew to hear spoon better. I smelled warm meat and onion. "Ask Boot for pencils and paper," spoon whispered.

"*Alleluia*," sang the radio box, "*praise Him!*"

"Chop!" went axe into the block. I didn't ask Boot or Sack for anything. I knew better. *You should know better, Hester. You are a big girl now.*

"I should know better," I whispered back to spoon.

"*Praise Him! Praise Him!*" sang the radio box.

"Chop chop!" went axe into the block.

Spoon lifted meat and potato from the pot as she stirred. "Ask Boot."

"But I am a big girl now," I whispered back.

"Ask him."

"But—"

"*Ask him.*"

After we'd eaten the stew Sack said that her back was giving her trouble and she was going to bed. Boot sat at the table making a matchstick boat in a bottle. Spoon lay clean and drying across the rack. I could see her from where I was sitting on the floor with Cat. "Ask now," said spoon.

"Now?"

"Yes, now."

"But—"

"*Now.*"

"Could I have a pencil and paper?" I asked Boot.

He looked up from his boat building; a matchstick shook between his fingers. "What?" he said.

"Could I have a pencil and paper?"

He waited. "Why don't you call me *daddy*, or *papa*? What is wrong with you? Every daughter calls her father *daddy* or *papa*. Why not mine?"

I looked at Boot, at his trousers and his white fingers holding the matchstick. There were some small dark hairs on the knuckles. I looked at his neck coming out of the top of his shirt. His neck had gray hairs, faint red lines, and some brown spots that looked soft like sponge. Why had they grown up out of his skin, those spots? What was inside them? Boot scratched at his shoulder. "Father, could I have a pencil and paper?" The circles of Boot's eyes filled with water that came from a deep well beneath his feet. He put down the matchstick—matchstick quick-whispered *thank you*—and came to me across the floor. He held my face in his hands, they smelled of stew and boat glue, and he kissed the top of my head. Then he went into the locked study. He came back with a pencil and some paper. The paper had blue lines running across. I had to hold back my hungry hands from grabbing.

"What are you going to do with them, Hester?" he asked. "Are you going to write me a letter?" His mouth curled up at the sides as he passed me the pencil and the paper. I lay across the floor and started to draw. I couldn't wait. Boot watched for a minute, then went back to the boat. "Don't make a mess," he said.

The pencil had me sailing on a spoon-boat, the way Noah did in the storm. I wore a skirt and a flower hat and I stood at the front of the spoon-boat. It was me who knew the way. We sailed through the hole in the bottle.

"I hope you've drawn a picture of me," said Boot, his mouth curling up again. "Show me." He bent down to where I lay on the floor and he looked at my picture. "What is all of this?" He shook his head. "I can let you have the pencils and paper for drawing as long as we clean up after ourselves." Then Boot took my spoon-boat and he turned it into a small ball. He put it in the kitchen bin with the bones and the dust. "You can have more later. It will be our secret." He put his finger to his mouth. "*Shhhhhh.*"

There are one-person secrets and there are two-person secrets. This was a two-person secret. Boot gave me pencils and paper for drawing when Sack's back gave her trouble and she had to take an early lie-down. Pencil spoke softly to me while I drew. She said, "I am your friend for eternity." I said, "What is eternity?" Pencil answered, "Where there are no walls or floors. Where it is light and you can hear the music of the wind." I drew eternity. It had stones and water and the wind blew. There was a house with pencil walls and there were spaces between every pencil so you could always visit the forbidden outside. "What do you do in eternity?" I asked pencil as I drew. "You become the eye of the world, you see it all, it goes into you, and when it goes into you it doesn't hurt. It shivers. You have wings." "Can you dance there?" "Yes, of course." I drew wings dancing with wings, lifting me up and spinning me into the eye of the world. "What do you eat in eternity?" I asked. Pencil said, "Apples." I filled the sky with apples.

Whenever I drew Boot was there. He sat at the table and put boats in bottles. After a while he looked at my drawings, shook his head, curled his mouth up at the sides, and said, "What a funny mess." Then he took my picture, made it a tiny ball of paper, and put it in the kitchen bin. I counted the little hand going around the face of the clock and I waited for the next time Sack had her back trouble, and I could draw again.

It was raining and Sack said it was too wet for washing. Cat and me couldn't look at the outside through the window from the couch arm. "Tomorrow will have to do," said Sack, and sneezed. I climbed up onto the couch arm anyway, and looked at the brown curtains. Sack said, "Get down off there." Boot came in. Sack blew her nose into a handkerchief. "I'd better check on Mother. Last time there was a downpour like this her chimney leaked."

"I can go," said Boot, touching her arm.

"No," said Sack, and pushed past him. "My mother doesn't recognize you."

"But you aren't well, Katherine."

"I'm well enough." She took her coat from the hook and wrapped her scarf around her cold neck. She sneezed again, then walked out the front door. I had never been out the front door because I was a source of shame and the thief of my mother's strength.

Now the house only had Boot in it. And me. "Who is 'my mother'?" I asked Boot.

"What?"

"Who is 'my mother'?"

"*Who is your mother*, what do you mean?"

"Who is she?"

"You know who your mother is, Hester." Boot shook his head because I was an aberration, then went into his study and locked himself inside. The doorway of Boot's study opened into the neck of a bottle and if you stepped through you stepped straight into the bottle and got stuck like the boats. Only Boot could come and go.

Water fell down onto the house. The sky rumbled. "Hester." Somebody called me. I went into the kitchen. "Hester, turn me." It was handle. Jesus beat the drum the way he did at the feasts. "Hester, I am your true friend. Turn me."

"But I should know better."

"Turn me," he said again.

"But—"

"*Turn me! Turn me! Turn me!*" I turned him. The back door opened to the forbidden outside. It was dark and wet; water poured from the home of the sun. Jesus beat the drum faster. I walked down through the wet grass. The hungry sky rumbled again. Tree was there, still reaching, but for what? There was no sun. I ran to her, to ask her. She was rough against my cheeks, her kisses rough on my lips. She said, "Pretty . . . beautiful."

"Tree, what do you reach for?" I asked, my mouth pressed close. I put my ear to her for an answer. There was nothing. "What are you reaching for, tree?" Still no answer. "Tree, talk to me, tell me what you reach for."

Her voice was a cooing pigeon. "I am reaching as high as I can."

"For what?"

"For all of the highest things."

"For eternity?"

"Yes, for eternity. Eternity is the highest of all."

Water fell down on my head. The world was a bath. I pulled off my clothes and my shoes and ran around the garden. A bright light turned on in the sky, then there was a crashing sound, and I shouted back as loud as I could. "Aaaaaahhhhh!" The grass was sharp under my feet; my feet prickled because they had insects running in circles inside them. Running and rubbing their wings together, calling and singing as I ran and laughed the devil's laugh. A dark shape moved down from the house toward me. It was Sack. Tree called, "Come here, climb me!" I jumped up to her lowest branches and tried to pull myself higher. My legs hung down. My feet of insects made them too heavy to lift. Sack had me by the back. She smacked my legs. "You'll be the death of me!" My feet broke open and the black insects came charging out from my toes. They ran up my legs, along my back, across my tum, and down onto Sack, who screamed. The insects covered us until there was no skin left. Rain fell. The sky lit up over our heads; I could see the flame fingers of the tree with the sky white and angry behind them. Tree shouted, "You will be the death of her!" and Sack pulled me back inside by my hair and arm, insects streaming from her body.

After that the back door was always locked. Handle stayed quiet when I passed. Sometimes I looked at him and there was a question in his wooden eye but I couldn't hear it, even with my ear pressed close I couldn't.

When I grew bigger my jobs were sweeping floors, mopping floors, cleaning between cracks, washing walls and clothes, dusting Our Savior, cleaning toilet with toilet brush, wood stacking, washing dishes, setting table with washed dishes, polishing forks and spoons. Prayer. Prayer was God washing me, stacking me, dusting me, sweeping me, mopping me, and hanging me out to dry. Prayer made pink cracks across my knees that hurt but I didn't stop. Once I did. Sack's voice was loud beside me, "*And God said take unto me my child, my heart, he that weepeth, knoweth not why he does but that God does move and when,*" and I stopped. I don't know why. I knew the words of the prayer but I stopped anyway. Sack kept going on her own and then she stopped too. She looked at me and I looked back. The pink spider under her eye waved his legs at me. Something special was going to happen.

"Sorry," I said.

"Get up," Sack said.

"Sorry," I said, and then I said it again: "Sorry."

"Too late for sorries." Sack took my hand and she pulled me up. I tried to pull my arm back to the part where Jesus beat the drum *beat beat beat*, but Sack wouldn't have it. "I won't have it, Hester, I won't have it!" She pulled harder again— "The more you pull, the worse it will be!"—so up I got and followed. She took me down the stairs, into the kitchen, through to the pantry, and opened a door in the floor I never knew was there, down some more stairs, and then we were in a dark room. She called up through the door in the floor, "John! John! Get down here and help me!"

Boot came down the stairs. "Yes, Katherine, what is it?"

"She needs to learn."

"Katherine, do you think, do you really think?"

"Would I be taking her arm? Would I be calling you like this?"

"No—no."

"Help me lift her to the table."

"I'm—I'm not sure." Boot's voice was stopping and starting.

"John, you lift her onto the table. Lift her. Lift her!" Sack's voice was loud. I kept quiet while Boot did as he was told. I saw a white shape in the faraway coming closer. Boot put his hands under my arms and lifted me *hup!* onto a table that was waiting. The wood of the table was warm under my feet. A bar hung down over the table like a swing, attached to the ceiling with ropes. More ropes dangled loose from each end of the bar. The dangling ropes were waiting for something to tie up. They wanted to bind a small animal.

The white shape was very close now—it was a big white bird. He stopped in front of me. "I am God the Bird," he said. God the Bird's wings were the same shape as the cracks in the ceiling, his beak was long and gold, he had a crown of stones, and his eyes were black lights. God the Bird flapped his wings, his gold beak close to my face. Table spoke up through my feet. "I am here, Hester, and I am your friend."

"What is a friend?"

"A friend gives you pictures."

Sack climbed up onto the table and tied my arms onto the bar. My arms were open wide like Christ on the cross. The bar ran across my back. If buckets hung from the bar I could have carried water. "Look at the walls, Hester, look at the company you keep!" she said close to my ear as she tied. There were pictures pasted to the walls of people hanging from their necks with rope. Other people in the pictures stood and looked. They were like the people who stoned Mary. Some of the people hanging had black bags over their faces so their eyes were hidden. There were pictures of ladies lying on pins, and pictures of ladies being stretched on wheels. In one picture a lady's head lay in a fruit basket. The eyes looked up to the sky where the Lord would not forgive. Sack climbed down and said, "Move the table now, John." Boot looked at me and I looked back. He scratched at his back as if a mouse was caught in his shirt. It was the eczema. It crawled across his back in search of water. "Move the table," said Sack. Boot moved the table and all of my body hung down by my arms like the company I kept. I could not feel my friend beneath my feet; my friend was gone. I was hanging.

God the Bird said, "Quiet now, Hester."

As Sack walked up the stairs table called to me from across the room. "Wait, little Hester, your time will come."

I hung there and God the Bird stayed with me. When he flapped his wings a breeze blew the hair from my eyes and dried my eyes and face. It cooled my hot wet body. God the Bird's beak was a smile. He made his wing do a wave. I couldn't wave back because my arm was tied to the bar; I hoped God the Bird knew. I told him *sorry* and then he flew up into the air over my head and the hanging room filled with blue sky and I didn't know where I went.

From the faraway blue I heard Boot say, "Do you think that's enough?"

"Take her down," said Sack. Boot untied me and I fell down onto the table but my arms tried to fly up there back to God the Bird. It made me smile. "Go upstairs," Sack said. I couldn't walk. I told my feet to make the steps but they wouldn't do the job. Boot picked me up in his arms and God the Bird flew in circles around me, his black eyes shining.

• • •

I woke up in my bed with hurting arms.

The next time Boot gave me pencil and paper I drew God the Bird carrying me on his wing to the land of the sun. I drew tree lifting from the ground. Dirt fell from her root onto the roof of One Cott Road as she lifted, covering it. I drew tree flying beside us with her flame hands flapping. She was coming too. Then I drew the company I kept standing in a circle around the house way below us. The black bags were off their heads so I could see their faces, but they didn't have eyes, only eyeholes. God the Bird had their eyes in his beak. He was carrying them to Jesus to eat at his feast.

I was washing a plate in the sink when Sack came and stood behind me. "Hester, stop what you are doing, I have something to show you." I kept washing the plate. There was sticky egg on the side. "Hester, did you hear me? I asked you to stop what you are doing." I washed over and over the egg. One bit of yellow sticky was left. It didn't want to leave. "Hester?" The plate was egg's friend. If the plate let go then egg would have nobody. "Hester." Sack put her arm on mine. I stopped cleaning the plate. Water dripped from the wet cloth onto the toe of my shoe. It left watermarks the shape of suns on the leather. Sack took my wet hand in her dry one. "Leave that in the sink," she said. I put the plate back. Egg and onion skin floated on top of the gray water. Sack led me out of the kitchen and I followed her up the stairs. "Come on." She pulled my hand to go faster.

We stood holding hands in the doorway of the room that would be mine when she said. The room wasn't empty anymore; it had my bed in it with a colored blanket on top that I hadn't seen before. The blanket was made of colored woolen squares. They were yellow, blue, purple, green, white, and red. "I knitted it," Sack said, "for you." On the wall was a picture of a lamb and a lion. They were lying together. The lamb was the mother of the lion. If there was something you wanted to know you asked the lamb. Cat jumped up on the bed and rolled onto her back on the colored blanket so her tum was up for tickling. "Funny cat . . ." Sack said, bending down and scratching Cat under the chin. I looked around the room; on the shelf were *The Abridged Picture Bible* and *Illustrated Hymns*. There was a flower in a cup; it was the same flower as the ones with the pink skirts that grew around tree. Above the shelf was Christ Our Savior. His arms were open wide and the blood on his dress was gone. There was a carpet on the floor with swirling leaves and a moon. Light came through the small window and poured onto the pillow.

"Do you like it?" Sack asked me. I didn't know what she wanted me to say or do. "It is your room now, Hester. From now on you will sleep in here. It is yours." She looked at me as if she was waiting for something. "Do you like it?" she asked again. What happened next I didn't want to happen, I didn't wish it. I cried. Sack stepped in and put her arms on me; they were hard arms, like the arms of a chair. "I am sorry for things," she said. My crying went into the hard of her arms, and stopped. Sack stood back, her arms full with my tears, and dabbed at her eye with a handkerchief. The pink spider waved and smiled underneath. "It is your room now. I always wanted a room of my own." She blew her nose into her handkerchief and then she was gone.

I stepped into the room that was mine. I was the only one there. If I put one foot wrong, nobody could see it.

The next time Boot gave me pencil and paper I drew the lamb riding on the back of the lion. Leaves grew around the moon. In my picture Christ Our Savior sang the hymn about the people dancing for joy, from *Illustrated Hymns*. He had the colored blanket around his shoulders. When he lay down to sleep it was in a room all of his own in a bed of dark.

I was drinking cat milk on my hands and knees when I heard a loud knock at the door. Sack said, "Upstairs, Het, upstairs and under the bed, go on! Up up up!" I ran upstairs, and bending I watched through the bars. A man with a round brown hat on his head stood outside One Cott Road.

"Mrs. Wakefield." The man put his hand out but Sack didn't take it.

"Yes?"

"I am from the Department of Welfare."

"Yes?"

"We have written to you but received no response. You left us no choice but to come to the house, as we advised that we would in our last letter."

"Well?"

"We believe you have a daughter, Mrs. Wakefield, and that she doesn't go to school."

Sack's eyes became two little blue fires that burned holes in hat man. "Yes, I have a daughter, and she has certain problems—mental problems. We teach her everything she needs to know at home."

Hat man wiped the shine from his face. "Nevertheless her condition will have to be assessed by an outside professional body—there might be a place for her in a special school. You may be entitled to some financial assistance."

"Do you think we don't know our own daughter?"

"I am not suggesting that you do not know your own daughter, Mrs. Wakefield, but—"

"Hester is not well enough to go to school."

"Your daughter will have to be tested—perhaps the outcome of those tests will indicate that she should stay home with you, in which case you could be eligible for some assistance."

"We don't want any assistance." From where I watched I felt the fires burning hotter in Sack. She wanted to give that hat man a turn in the hanging room—maybe she'd want to give me a turn in there too. It was time for me to hide under the big bed.

I heard the front door close and Sack coming quickly up the stairs. Hat man was gone. Sack came into the room, bent over, and looked under the bed. I made myself small and flat as the hidden pencil but the fires in her eyes lit up the darkness and she saw me hiding. She reached in and grabbed me by the arm. I took hold of her leg with her foot in her hard shoe and I held on tight. "Let go of me, Hester!" I didn't let go. She kicked and wriggled and her shoe got me smack in my throat. She pulled me out. "I was too old to have you—I wasn't strong enough!"

That night I lay in my bed of dark. Hat man came from the forbidden outside. Did he come from the same place that Boot went to every day? Did he come from the same place as the eggs and porridge? What was *school*? That night my wooden bed sang me to sleep. *Yahweh's people dance for joy, praise Him praise Him!*

For the day of the tests Sack sewed me a dress, tight across the top, with a row of buttons. Buttons are small circles that hold a dress together. Without buttons the dress is a loose cape that lets you fly. You have to have buttons. Sack brushed my hair—each stroke pulled at my wicked knot—and tied it back. Sack went into her room and came out in a gray skirt with tiny flowers that grew along the edges. I had not seen that skirt before. Her shirt had little white grapes that grew up around her neck and down her back. Her shoes were shiny with an *up* at the back. Sack walked around the house on little boxes *tap tap tap*. There was a gold chain hanging on her throat, but Jesus wasn't there, only the cross of his home.

Boot took my hand and we three walked out the front door. I could see all of the forbidden outside under the gray of the sky and all of it shone with the light of eternity.

Boot took me down to his chariot but it was different than the chariots in *The Abridged Picture Bible*. Its wheels were black and it had a brown roof and brown doors. The chariots in my Bible had flying red ribbons, golden doors, and spikes coming from the wheels to stop the other chariots. Thick-legged Romans rode the chariots in my Bible. They wore helmets and whipped the horses in front, shouting, "Win! Win!" Sack wanted me to lie across the back seat. She pushed me down. "Try and sleep."

I lay across the back seat and made up a song to the rumbling music of the chariot. It was about Abel and what he did to Cain when his father was out. Abel knew it was wrong but he did it anyway, he did it over and over with a stick, he couldn't stop himself. He did it again and again, it didn't matter that Cain was shouting, *No, please don't, please don't, Abel, please don't*, Abel kept on doing it anyway. He wanted to see blood on Cain's knees. After a long time of driving Boot stopped the chariot. "We're here. Wake up, Hester." Boot touched my arm. "Time to get out."

Sack turned around from the front seat and pinched me short and quick. "Behave in there." The pink spider held a fist up at me. I climbed out of the brown chariot and Boot and Sack took a hand each. I saw two dogs from Jesus and the marketplace. They chased each other and barked. Water came from a pipe and wet the grass. There were many trees and houses. In front of the houses were squares of grass with bars for hanging and plastic buckets. The road was full of chariots without spikes speeding past. I wanted to run and sing my song loud. The madness of the world was infecting me.

We walked down a path into a big box house. There were flowers growing all along the sides of the path. They were white with yellow stripes. The flowers rested in beds of leaves. I wanted to stop and look closer to see if there were ants and if they lived under the flowers but Boot and Sack pulled me along. *Tap tap tap* went the box shoes of Sack as she walked. My dress was tight across my chest. We went inside the building. There was a room full of chairs with a jar of flowers in the corner. A lady sat behind a desk. Her lips were red and shining and around her neck was colored glass. She smiled at Boot and Sack and me. "Please take a seat, the doctor will be with you shortly."

We sat in three seats. Sack let go of my hand but Boot didn't. There was a pile of paper books on a table in the corner. If I turned my head I saw a queen on the front. She was not the same as the queen in *The Abridged Picture Bible*; she didn't have as many clothes on. Sack did a sharp turn with her head at me and I stopped looking at the queen because it was wrong. That's why Adam ran so fast.

A man came through a door. He walked toward us with his arm held out. Boot shook the hand. "Mr. and Mrs. Wakefield?"

He looked down at a paper he was holding. "Come inside, Hester." Boot and Sack wanted to come into the room with me but the man who looked like hat man but more smiling and no hat said, "Just Hester this time, please." Sack's mouth went as straight as the fence outside One Cott Road. Boot patted her hand and in I went.

The man took me into a room. There were a lot of colored things in boxes. There were yellow chariots made of plastic, there were blocks and bells and dolls made of wool and a soft mouse and a white rabbit with pink ears, and books with shiny pictures of trains, clouds, and a man with a red nose and shoes too big for him, round at the top. There was a pile of paper and pencils. One of the pencils was green. The man with the smile asked me to point at a circle and a triangle and a line. He asked me to put the same things together and take the different things away. He asked me which way the lines were going. He said, "Which one is different?" He said, "What is the biggest?" and "Hold up your fingers when you see the light go on." He sat me on a bed and looked close at my eyes and ears with a torch tied to his head. He held up a picture of a man, a lady, and two children sitting on a blanket eating bread with cheese. The man said, "Can you tell me about this picture, Hester?"

"They are outside. They are eating. Christ has blessed the bread," I told him. He held up another picture. "That's Noah in the boat that got out of the bottle. The Lord is sending his punishment out of the clouds. It's making them wet," I told him. The man smiled. He didn't have *The Abridged*

Picture Bible at home under his bed. He needed Hester to show him.

Next the man held up a picture of many beasts. "What is your favorite animal, Hester?"

I pointed to the cat. "Meeeee-oooowww!" The man smiled wide.

"Then you won't like this picture." He held up a picture of a cat being chased by a dog.

"Dog wants to eat cat for his dinner!" This time the man laughed. *Did Sack hear from outside? Was her ear pressed to the door?*

"Yes, I think you are right there," he said. He held up a picture of three girls jumping over rope. The sun shone on their heads. "I think these girls look happy. What do you think, Hester?"

I looked at the picture for a long time. "They are outside. They can jump high, they can laugh, nobody can hear them. They are happy, they are outside, and they are friends."

"Yes, yes. I agree with you entirely," the man said. I looked across at the pencils. He pushed the pencils and paper toward me. "It looks like you want to draw, Hester."

I took my wish and I drew the leaves on the path. They were growing all around the wheels and through the windows of Boot's chariot. The green leaves grew into the chariot and then they grew around Sack and they grew around Boot, over their heads, around their legs and wrists and into Sack's mouth and then into my mouth and then into Boot's mouth so nobody could talk anymore.

"Would you like to go to school, Hester?"

"What is school?"

"It's a place where children go every day to be with each other and to learn new things. School is a place of discovery, or it should be."

"The wickedness of man is great on the earth," I told him. I wasn't sure that the man knew.

"I can't argue with you there." He smiled. "Hester, at school you would be with other children your own age. You would have to be away from your mother and father every day. Are you ready for that?"

School is a place of discovery. A discovery was what Pharaoh's daughter made when she found Moses in the reeds. That's how she saved Moses from drowning. I nodded a yes. The man smiled again, stood up, and took my hand. I waited for him to throw my picture away. He said, "Why don't you take it with you?" I didn't know the answer he wanted so I left it there.

I followed the man back to where Boot and Sack were waiting. There were no fires in Sack's eyes now. There was cold water, deep, without waves. If you threw a stone into one of her eyes it would sink forever; there would be no bottom for the stone to reach. It would always be sinking. The smiling man talked to Boot and Sack. I stayed sitting on my chair, my eye trying to see the queen with no clothes, though it was a sin. Soon the man shook the hand of Boot again and we left the building.

When we were back in the chariot, Sack cried, "What did you tell him? How did you betray me?"

Boot said, "It will be all right, Kathy—let's just get home." Was the man with the smile still there after I left?

When we got back to One Cott Road Boot didn't hold my hand as we walked up the path. He was half-carrying Sack. She was small and folded and falling against him like cloth. "Go on, Hester, get inside," he said. "Put the kettle on while I help your mother to bed."

The next morning broom and me were sweeping the hallway when we heard crying. We followed the sobs into the living room, where we found Sack in the fireplace—no fire, just ashes. The ashes were on her cheeks and her hands, legs, and arms. She had no clothes on. She was curled up like Cat when she's sleeping but Cat doesn't cry. I stood with broom in my hand. Broom asked, "How do you sweep a fireplace with a Sack inside?" We listened to the crying. "Broom, stay here," I said. I let him go and he fell to the floor behind me. "Ouch!" I walked to Sack; I bent down into the fireplace and I touched her leg where the knee was. Sack stopped crying; she turned her head, all black, all sooty, and she looked at me like I was a new person in the house, a bright stranger she might wish for—not Hester, her source of great shame, not *this*.

I said, "God forgives our sins."

Sack grabbed me and pulled me into the fireplace. Now there were ashes on *my* dress, *my* socks, *my* elbows. Sack cried on me, her tears running down my neck, arms, and face. I grew heavy and sodden with her tears. I needed a hand to wring me out. "God might forgive me but you never could—you—you shouldn't!" she cried. "I am going to lose you, I know it—it's coming, it's coming." Those were the words—hard to hear with so much crying—but Hester has big ears and she heard.

Sack cried on me a while longer and then she said, "Get up and sweep like I told you." I got out and picked up broom, who was lying there waiting, and together we swept the ashes while Sack went and washed hers down the sinkhole.

The fire was hot in the kitchen. The dishes were stacked and I was drying. Spoon was whispering something to me but I couldn't hear her properly. Boot said, "Hester, tomorrow you are going to school." He sat at the table and looked into my eyes. "It is not what we want but there is nothing we can do about that. We know you belong at home. You are not the same as other children. Your mother is not well, Hester, we mustn't upset her."

Spoon whispered, "What is school?"

Chair and table answered, "A place of discovery."

Sack pulled the tight dress with the row of buttons over my head. "I want to know everything, Hester. I want to know what you do there." Her hair came down over her face; some of it covered an eye, but I could still see the pink spider. I wondered if Sack could see with that too. Would the things she saw when she looked with her spider-eye be different than the things she saw with her blue ones? Would she be able to see, with her spider-eye, the invisible web, its sticky strands? She pressed me to her. I smelled sugar and toilet. "Don't believe them," she said.

Boot took me down to the chariot and opened the back door. "Lie down in there, Hester."

"Why?" I asked him.

"Don't ask your questions now that your mother isn't here. Just do as you're told. I have to get to work." I climbed into the back seat, lay down, and listened to the chariot drive us away from One Cott Road.

I made up songs as we drove and I sang them to the music of the chariot. In one song Abraham rode on a camel; the camel had red socks on his paws. In another song Jesus did a dance on the water and everybody clapped. "More!" they shouted. "More, Jesus, give us more! We want more! More! More! Give us more! More! More! Dance your dance on the water again! More! More! More! More!" Soon Boot said, "We are here, Hester." He stopped the chariot and turned to me from the front. "Keep your secrets to yourself or else there'll be trouble at home. It's time to go—up you get." I sat up, and Boot got out of the car and opened my door. The forbidden outside lit up so I could see all its secrets glowing. The world was in a very bright light. It was the sun, warm and yellow over the trees and chariots and paths and flowers and fences and houses and over the other children running and laughing who I was not the same as. A whistling wind blew my hair that Sack had tied tight so that it came loose around my face, then it blew the trees, it blew the dogs and the houses. Everything lifted up into the air. I lifted too. Dogs, houses, chariots—we all blew up closer to the sun, my dress went over my head, my mouth blew open, and a laugh blew out.

Boot and me walked up to the school. It was bricks with porches going all around. There were rows of windows with white crosses in the middle. My feet shook in my brown hard shoes with a lace. My feet would have run away if it wasn't for the lace. My chest pushed against the dress and the row of buttons. Jesus beat the drum from the feasts *beat beat beat*. The light over all things burned my eyes. A lady with hair in soft circles and pink on her lips came down the porch steps toward us. Her dress was made of green and blue wool. She was in a cloud of grass. She said, "I will be your teacher. My name is Mrs. Dane—it's Hester, isn't it?"

I said, "I won't tell one lie," and the smile my teacher made turned her face into a bridge for walking. She said, "That's a good start, then." I let go of Boot's hand.

"Good-bye, Hester. I will be here to collect you at the end of the day," he said. I walked up the path with my teacher and when I turned back to see Boot, him and his chariot had been blown away by the whistling wind.

My teacher opened a door and took me into a room. There were colored drawings on the wall; some had feathers, some had wool, and one had sticks. The windows around the room did not have curtains. You could see the forbidden outside through every window. The room was the same color as the sun shining through.

There were lots of tables and chairs and children who I was not the same as. They looked at me from the rows of tables and chairs with eyes like insects. My teacher said, "You can sit beside Mary." Mary had a lip twisted up with a nose. She moved over and I sat down.

One boy whispered, "Hey, fatty."

Another boy whispered, "Fatty boomsticks," and somebody laughed the devil's language.

My teacher stood at the front. Her voice was from my song; it had a soft bell and questions. Everybody listened. Sometimes the other children put a hand up high, my teacher pointed, and then they said, "Africa," and "continent," and "Eskimos." She took a book from her desk. "Time to go on with our story," she said. "Who remembers where we were up to?"

"David was building his own balloon to fly in," one boy called out.

"He had to bring food for a year because he was going to fly across the world," a girl said.

"He'd see polar bears, lions, and eagles!"

"The balloon was pink and yellow silk with stripes!"

"Flames came out and that's what made it fly!" Everyone was calling out over the top of each other.

"David was going in search of his—"

"Father!"

"Who made magic buttons."

"Sugar buttons!"

"Magic sugar buttons! That's why they kidnapped him. He had the power!"

"All right, all right, I see you do remember. Quiet now." Mrs. Dane smiled and opened the book. She began to read. *"David checked the ropes. It was the first time he had seen the balloon in the light of day. How it glowed, beckoning him . . ."* Every ear in the room grew wide to take in the one voice of Mrs. Dane. *"The balloon's great panels of pink and yellow silk billowed. The moment had finally arrived. The journey could at last begin."* I turned my head. Outside the window David rose up in his balloon, beckoning me.

My teacher read and read. The world spread beneath David and me, a living map.

"It is now time for your playlunch," said my teacher. "You can hear more of the story tomorrow." The other children moaned; nobody wanted the story to end. Then there was the sound of all the chairs and tables scraping back and I followed everybody out of the room.

The others knew where to go. They ran out into the flat black under the forbidden sky and they kept running in all directions around me. I saw a tree with a long flat bench under it and so I walked there and sat down. I watched the other children hang upside down from colored bars, swinging and screaming. One ran like the horse that pulled the chariot. Two girls climbed a table and sang and laughed. The devil's language filled the school. Mary stood alone and looked at me from across the flat black. I could see into her eyes all the way from where I stood there was so much room for me inside them.

A loud bell rang and everybody went back into the room. A boy said, "What did you eat for playlunch, fatso, your brother?" Children laughed the devil's language, then my teacher came in and the room went quiet. Who was my brother? Where did he live? What did he eat?

"Spelling books out, please." My teacher walked to where I sat beside Mary. "I know you don't have any books here yet. And that you haven't been taught any reading and writing, so we'll do the best we can." Then she said to the others, "Go to page three and do the next spelling list." Then she showed me an A and asked me to draw one. I drew one line up, one line down, and one line across. It was the beak of God the Bird. "A is for apple," said my teacher, and drew an apple.

When she had gone back to the front of the room Mary looked at my A. "A is for arse," she said.

It was lunchtime. I went to the bench again. I ate Sack's cheese and I ate Sack's bread and the boards on the bench sang a song from *Illustrated Hymns* up through my backside. "*He gives His gifts, He gives them in plenty.*"

After lunch my teacher put paper sheets on the middle table, then gave me a brush. "Here," she said, "for painting." She filled up white plates with all the colors of the world. The colors shone like wet stars on a plate sky. The brush was made of wood, like spoon and tree. I never held anything as tight before. The brush tickled the tips of my fingers when it spoke. "I am your friend, Hester."

"Will you give me pictures?"

"I will give you everything." Everyone put their brushes in the paint and then I put my brush in the blue paint. I put the brush, wet with the blue paint, to the paper and Sack's blue eye blinked at me from the white page; a tear came slowly from its corner. As I painted, dipping in all the colors, brush spoke louder, making my fingers tickle all the way to the bone. "I am your friend, paint, paint!" The words made me laugh. My teacher said, "What's funny, missy?" I stopped my laugh because it came from the devil somewhere inside that I couldn't put a finger on, but I kept painting.

I painted one blessing, one bird, one prayer, one obedience, one cat, one throne, one shoe, one creeping creature, one holiness, one lie, one cross, one window, and one sink. Last I painted God the Bird flying through a cloud of grass. My teacher was there, feeding him apples.

My teacher touched my hand. I stopped painting and brush went quiet. My teacher kept her hand on mine and she said, "Good work, Hester." The neck of me grew long, my body stretched and filled with air, my legs grew tall, my ears pulled wide apart from each other as the word *good* bounced around and around in the new space inside of me.

When school was finished for the day, Boot was there waiting in his chariot on the street. When he saw me coming he got out and opened the door in the back. "I can't pick you up every day like this," he said. "I can't leave work early again. You are going to have to catch the bus with the others. Kathy won't like it, but there's nothing I can do." I lay across the back seat and the friends that gave me pictures were there when I closed my eyes and I wondered if David had found his father the button maker yet.

Sack was in bed when I got home. Boot told me to be quiet in case she was sleeping. He went up to her room with tea. When he came back down he said, "You are to cut up the vegetables for the dinner. When you have done that you are to go up and see your mother and tell her what happened at school today."

I cut up the carrot and the cabbage—the corn I couldn't cut because it was in small circles with flat bottoms. All the time I was cutting I looked around for where the A was. There was one in carrot, two in cabbage, and none in corn. When I finished cutting I went upstairs to see Sack. She was sitting up in her bed with the back pillow behind her. She looked at me. "Traitor," she said. I didn't know what she wanted me to do next so I stood there, waiting. "Come here," she said. I went there. Her hair was still covering one eye and there was wet on her face. Her white hands went around me like rope.

"Let me look at you." Did she see the paintings I made? Did she see Mary across the flat black? Did she see the color of the schoolroom?

"What did you do, what did they tell you?" she asked. I didn't know what she wanted me to say so I didn't say anything. "*What?*" I still didn't know what she wanted me to tell her. If you don't know how can you say? The rope of her arm tightened. "Who will you become?" She pulled her hair back from the eye. "Go to your room." That's what I did because I knew that's what she wanted. I sat on the floor and looked for A's in *The Abridged Picture Bible*. I found one in the lamb and some in Abraham and one in the head of John the Baptist. Sack didn't come downstairs for dinner. Boot and me ate it together. The only sound was our forks and our knives talking to each other as they scraped across the plates.

"Holding down the meat is a hard job," scraped my fork.

"Not as hard as cutting it," scraped back Boot's knife.

After dinner I washed the dishes and did the sweeping. "Broom?" I said.

"Yes," answered broom, *sweep sweep*.

"I made a new friend today."

"Good," he said, *sweep sweep*.

"And I painted."

"What did you paint?" *sweep sweep*.

"My teacher."

"You like her?"

"Yes."

"Good." *Sweep sweep.*

After dinner Boot held a bottle up so the light was behind it. "It's a trick, Hester. How did the boat get in there, is that what you are asking yourself?"

The next morning when we got to the school Boot told me that I had to catch a bus home. He said it was called *Mill Park Bus.* He showed me where to get on it. I said, "What is a bus?"

Boot shook his head and pointed to a long box on wheels. "That. Your teacher will tell you when it goes. I've spoken to her."

My teacher drew numbers on the blackboard. I knew about counting. Boot showed me how the little hand goes around, past the three and the nine and up to the twelve. My teacher showed what you have left if you take some away. She asked me, "Hester, do you know the answer?" I didn't know what she wanted me to say so I said nothing. When she turned back to numbers on the board, one boy leaned close. "You're dumber than my little sister, fatty. You don't know anything." Mary leaned across me and the heat from Mary went around me like the cape that Jesus wore on the coldest night in the garden, the one before the judgment, when he slept in a cave. She whispered to the boy, "Your little sister eats shit."

My teacher put me in a reading pair with Judith. Judith had two white ribbons tied around two tails of yellow hair.

We sat on the floor with the book open and Judith pointed at the ant marks across the page with her finger. Her fingernail had chipped pink paint. Judith told a slow story about the boy and the house and the ball and the dog and the mother. Each black ant word went past the chipped pink paint, into her finger, through her hand, up her arm and neck, and out her mouth to me. That was a story. When Judith told it I closed my eyes and she gave me pictures. I saw the dog jumping, the boy chasing, and the house with the two windows and the mother saying, "Come inside." The dog had a patch on his eye. It was my wish to tell a story too. I put my finger on the ant marks but they stayed where they were. My teacher came over and said, "Judith, have another turn. Hester, we have a way to go yet." What is *a way to go*?

My teacher said, "Tidy time, class." We had to pick things up from the floor. I sat on the carpet and picked up all the things that were not carpet. Dust, dirt, string, and pencil shavings. The more I picked up the more I saw. My teacher came to me. "That's enough now, Hester. The area is clean." But I could see more. I kept passing my hand over the carpet; more bits of dust came into my hand. "Hester, that's enough, it's free reading time. You can go and look at picture books in the library section." My hand burned from the prickling carpet but there was more dirt coming all the time. It was my chore to pick it up. My teacher came down close to me, she put her hand over mine, and she said, "It is clean now, thank you." My teacher's voice was a soft bell. It rang with a song in my ear as I walked into the library section.

At playlunch Mary came to me with her hand stuck out. There was an orange in it. "Have some," she said. I didn't take any. She held the orange up in the air over our heads. "It's a juicy sun," she said. She peeled back the orange coat from the orange and the middle was wet with white spider web all around it.

She took a piece of the little sun and put it in her mouth. Orange water dripped from one corner. "Want a piece of the sun?" she asked me. In *The Abridged Picture Bible* Eve took the red apple and met the snake. Mary held the orange piece out to me. The snake hissed and bit Eve in the neck and it was the end of freedom. "Have some!" said Mary. I took the orange piece from Mary's hand. I put it in my mouth and waited for the end of freedom. Orange water jumped through the air as I chewed. The sun shone inside my mouth. Mary smiled and her lip that was twisted up with her nose smiled too. The bell rang and we walked back into the schoolroom swallowing orange.

My teacher told me to paint when the other children not the same as me did spelling and numbers. She gave me the brush and the plate of paint and said, "You paint what you want to." I painted my brother and the boy's little sister and David in the balloon. My teacher never put my paintings in the kitchen bin. She said, "Take them home. Mary will catch the bus with you." I waited with Mary. We stood under a small roof.

Around us boys said "crazies" and "freaks." Mary pushed her face forward. "Get fucked, you stinking cunts," she said, and the boys turned away. Mary looked at me and snorted air through her nose that twisted up with her lip. Soon the bus came and I followed Mary on. It was hot with rows of children laughing the devil's language. "Move over for the crazies," they said.

Mary said, "Fuck off," and then we sat on a seat together and Mary pointed at the streets where she rode her scooter with the dogs. "What's a scooter?" I asked. Mary held her two hands in fists and pretended to turn a corner. "One of those, you know?"

Mary said she used to have a dog called Ace of Spades and a dog called Whiskey because her dad's a cardie and a drinker but then the dogs ate the neighbors' chickens and Sissy's rabbit so her dad took the dogs to the dump and gave them the bullet. She said she didn't have dogs anymore but there were frogs in the forgotten pond and one was her pet. His name was Green and maybe one day he would talk.

I looked through the window and saw water from a long pipe spray through the air and behind it a hook of colors made of steam from the kettle. Mary said, "It's a rainbow, make a wish!"

"How do you make a wish?" I asked.

"You close your eyes and you wish it. You see it coming true. Hurry! Before the rainbow is gone." I closed my eyes and I wished it. I saw it coming true.

"What did you wish for?" Mary asked me when I opened my eyes. "You can tell me, it won't break the power."

"I wished for the frog to talk."

"He will one day, we just have to wait." The bus turned the corner onto Cott Road. "You have to get off here, Mrs. Dane told me."

Through the window I saw Sack waiting. She was wearing her shoes with the *up* at the back but her gown with the gray roses was the same. Her arms were folded across her body and she was looking in all the bus windows for me. The Lord held her face in a tight pinch between his finger and thumb. I waved through the window and the Lord let go of Sack's face as I stepped onto the street. I wanted to stay and wave good-bye to Mary but Sack turned me around and we walked fast down Cott Road. On both sides of the road were big squares of tall grass where houses might have been. One Cott Road was at the end with no more streets leading off. It was a house on its own. I was the friend of One Cott Road and so were handle, broom, and axe. But nobody else.

My paintings hid in the side of my schoolbag. They were pressed close to each other in the dark of the pocket. When I went into my room I took them out and hid some of them in the pages of *The Abridged Picture Bible*, some in the pages of *Illustrated Hymns*, and some under my sheet so when I moved in the night my paintings spoke to me *crackle crackle*. My paintings were a secret and secrets grow big if you leave them. My paintings slid out of the pages of *The Abridged Picture Bible* and *Illustrated Hymns* in the middle of the night. White paper birds with painted wings flapped around my room. They hovered over me, cooing and roosting on the headboard.

• • •

"It is autumn," said my teacher, "the time when the leaves fall. Go out into the playground and collect one leaf each." We ran around the black flat in the autumn sun that was mixed with cold. My leaf lay on her back beside the school fence. She had a whole tree inside her. When we got back into the class my teacher gave us paper you could see through. "For tracing," she said. We put our leaves under the tracing paper and with a pencil we traced the leaf onto the paper. Then we cut out the leaf with little scissors that had an orange handle. "Write your name on the leaf," said my teacher. She came and wrote my name on my leaf for me. My teacher hung the leaves on a paper tree. I looked at everybody else's leaves and each one held a whole tree inside it too. The wind came through the window and the names did a dance. Mine danced too, the same as everybody else's.

My teacher told a story about an elephant sitting on an egg. An elephant has a leg for a nose and is a friend of everybody. The egg cracked and an elephant with wings came out. It could fly and remember everything. If you remember everything then it stays and grows inside of you so you can tell it and have it back again. Elephants remember what got stolen and they remember the thief, but only some people do. "It is a story of great faith," said my teacher.

At lunch Mary said, "Come with me to the puddle where the frog lives."

"What's a frog?" I asked.

"Come and see." The puddle was deep like a sea, with a white bag and a floating shoe.

"This is the puddle," said Mary.

"What's a frog?" I asked.

"A frog is a green thing that sticks and jumps and talks to you. Frogs have the oldest song—older than birdsong. That's what nobody knows." We waited for the frog in the puddle. We put our feet in. Mary pointed at my legs with a stick. "What are the marks?"

I said, "The world is full of wickedness."

Mary said, "You're my first friend here." We waited for the frog until the bell rang and Mary said, "Next time he'll come, we just have to wait."

My teacher said, "Bring in something from your home that you'd like to share with the others, and tell us its story. Something that is important to you."

The next day Tim brought in two small men with hats and sticks. "They're soldiers from my grandfather," he said. "My grandfather fought in the war. His brother Sam went too but Sam didn't come back, only my grandfather did. Now my grandfather lives with us and sometimes he takes me to the movies. We eat whatever we like because he's got a sweet tooth."

Sarah brought in a purple plum. "It grew on a tree in our garden," she said. "My father makes jam. He never cooks anything else, but every year he makes jam from these plums and it ends up everywhere—even on the walls—because he's messy, but it's not jam for bread, it's jam for ice cream."

Jane brought in a stone with circles and a hole. "It's from the beach and if you put your ear to it you can hear it. We went to the beach last Christmas and I went out deep with my uncle Peter and he showed me how to ride a wave all the way in. Uncle Peter used to be a lifeguard and he's seen sharks. He said that a shark gave him such a fright that he was even scared to take a bath after that."

What story did I want to tell when it was my turn? Cat wrapped herself around my leg, but I couldn't bring Cat because she moved and wriggled and did what she wanted. I lay on my bed and looked around the walls of my room. The paintings went *crackle crackle* beneath me when I moved. I pulled out a painting of God the Bird.

The next day it was my turn. My teacher smiled at me. "What about you, Hester, what have you brought for us?" I stood up slowly. Somebody said, *Dumb arse.* I walked past the desks to the front of the class. I held up the painting of God the Bird. He was flying around my head where I hung. "He'll talk to you when you're hanging."

A cloud of quiet came down over the room. "Thank you, Hester." My teacher's lips closed in a tight smile.

"He comes to me when I am hanging for my punishment."

"Thank you, Hester, that is enough," my teacher said, no smile now.

"He talks. He says, *It will be all right, it will be all right.*" Nobody in the room spoke or moved. The cloud of quiet held them. "He has a black beak, he could peck out an eye if he wanted. He could put in his beak and pull out the eye and behind it there'd be nothing. Nothing! *Peck peck peck!* He comes when I hang. He says—"

"Thank you, Hester, that's enough!" my teacher snapped.

"He comes when Sack hangs me."

"Next please," said my teacher, as she turned away. "Christopher, have you got something to show us?"

When I came home Sack was on her knees wiping out the shelves. A cup of tea, undrunk, sat on the table. "It's never over," she said into the dark of the cupboard. She turned around to me. "Well? What happened?"

The story of my day burst out of me in the devil's language left unspoken too long. "My name did a dance."

"What?"

"On a tree."

"What dance? What tree?"

"A windy dance on a paper tree." I lifted my arms, pointed my toes, and danced around the kitchen like the leaf with my name—around the table, over the chairs, and past the window.

Sack threw her tea at me. It burned but not much because Sack only liked her tea warm, not hot. I stood still as I dripped. My dance was finished. Sack poured another cup of warm tea.

When I woke up today I was lying at the bottom of the stairs. I don't know why I woke up at the bottom of the stairs. I had sore knees, sore elbows, and a sore neck. Stairs were for climbing up and down, stairs were for falling, stairs were punishment and the way to my room. Boot wanted Sack to let me be. "Kathy, can you let her be now?"

"Are you telling me—her mother?"

"I don't think she understands."

"Then she has to learn. It's not your business." He left us then and we went back to learning, me with a black bag over my eyes and the hard floor making cracks in my knees.

Mary and me ate our lunch together under the tree. Mary only had an apple. She said, "Can I have some of yours?" I gave her my bread. Mary tore some off and gave back the rest. We ate the bread, then Mary climbed up to the first branch of the tree, hooked her knees over, and hung down. "I'm a flying fruit bat!" Her skirt fell over her head and a squeal mixed with laughter came out from under her skirt. She swung as she hung. "Come on, Hester!" she said, pulling her skirt back down. Her face was red. I climbed slowly up. I was shaking. "Come on, fruit bat!" said Mary. I shook in every part as I hooked my knees over. "Don't be scared, little fruit bat," said Mary. Slowly I let myself down beside her until I hung. The world was upside down so that the floor was made of clouds. Mary bit into her apple, then took the apple piece from her laughing mouth and fed it to me as we swung. Sweet apple filled my mouth. An eternity of clouds spread at my feet.

"Hester, there is a new chore for you to do now that you are bigger." Boot stood in the kitchen behind me while I dusted window ledges with the rag. "You are old enough to go out-side now, and chop the wood for the wood stove." He opened the back door for me and I saw tree and the grass and around the corner the line for hanging clothes. It was the forbidden outside. Boot walked to where axe leaned, taking a rest against the wall, and lifted him high, then he let him fall into wood, who waited on the block. Wood said, "Don't!" and "No!" but axe went down anyway. He had to; it was his chore.

"It is the weight of the axe itself that chops the wood, it takes less strength than you think," Boot said. "See the cuts already there?" He touched the black cuts with his finger. "That is where the axe should fall." I followed the cuts; I let the head of axe fall into them so that wood came apart around the block.

"That's right, Hester. And then you pile the wood up and bring enough inside to fill the wood box." Boot watched me chop. "What do they say to you at that place?" he asked me. I didn't say anything because I didn't know what answer he wanted. "It doesn't matter what they say, it is your mother and father you listen to."

"Why are you my father?"

Boot shook his head at me and went inside.

Axe and me went slow (I had to watch him or he missed the wood and tried for my foot). While we chopped axe sang a slow-chopping song into the cuts *chop chop chop, yes yes yes, more more more, chop chop chop, yes yes yes, more more more.* I carried the pieces chopped and ready into the kitchen. They lived in a box. It was quiet and dark in the box for them. They slept and dreamed about Hester and axe and how much it hurt to be chopped.

I opened the red door of the wood stove. Fire called out, "I'm hungry, Hester," while he did his leaping dance. I took a wood from the box and I put him in. The fire made my hands hot if I got too close. I watched the fire eat up the wood. Wood called out for me, "Hester, help, help! It hurts!" but how could Hester help? It was my chore to keep that hungry fire hot and flaming.

Mary and me waited for the frog at the puddle. Some days the puddle was bigger than others. There were always different things floating. I pointed with a stick and said, "What's that, Mary?"

She said, "A chip packet."

I said, "What's that, Mary?"

She said, "A fizzy drink can." We bent down close to the puddle and I stirred with my stick as if the puddle was soup. Then Mary said, "I had no friends because when I came out the doctor had to cut my lip from my nose. He did it on purpose," she said, "so the air had a hole to come through and if I didn't have the hole I'd be six feet under—but it means I don't have any friends." She threw a stone into the puddle, then looked at me. "Until now." The water moved out in circles getting bigger.

The next day we came and the puddle was gone. "Do you want to wait for the frog at a different place?" I nodded a yes.

"Follow me." I followed Mary behind the school. She held the wire in the fence up. "Crawl under." I crawled under and Mary said, "Now you hold it for me." I held the wire up and it cut a line of blood into my hand but I didn't let the wire cut Mary. We were in the world outside the school. We crossed a road empty of chariots and buses and then we were on grass at the top of a hill. At the bottom were trees and bush. We started to run down the hill. Mary was laughing. She threw herself onto the grass. "I'm a ball!" she shouted, and rolled. My song sang, I lay down and made myself into a ball too. Mary and me were two balls rolling. The world was turning circles, full up with our laughing sounds. At the bottom Mary said, "Come on, we're going to the creek."

"What's a creek?"

Mary shouted over her shoulder as she ran, "How come you don't know anything?" Branches whipped at our cheeks and knees as Mary and me ran along a winding trail through the bush. Faster and faster we ran, jumping over stones and fallen trees. The sky above us, the bush around us, the rocky ground under our feet all called, *Faster, Mary and Hester, faster, go go go!*

When the trail ended we stood breathing hard and looking at a rushing shining snake of water hissing its way between the trees. We went close to the water. "Does it bite like the serpent?" I asked Mary, between breaths.

"It doesn't bite, it wets," she said, putting her hand in and splashing me. The water was cold on my cheek. "Come on, froggy, come on, froggy," she whispered to the water.

"Come on, froggy, come on, froggy," I whispered too. We waited. I heard the snake of water moving, I heard birds and trees. I listened for the oldest song. Mary took off her shoes and put her toes into the water. I did too. Dark wet dirt came up between our toes. "Imagine if soap was made of dirt," said Mary, and washed up her legs with the dirt soap. I did too. It made my white legs brown. We ran along the creek in socks of mud. Mary kicked her feet in the water. Water sprayed up; I saw the world through water—loose, without edges.

We sat on the cool grass beside the creek and waited for the frog. After a while of quiet waiting I said to Mary, "I don't want the frog to come."

"Why not?" she asked me.

"Because then you'll say, 'That's the frog, now you've seen it, time to go back.'"

"When we do see the frog, we'll run away with him. We'll ride on his back and he'll sing us his song. But now it's time to go. Lunch will be over soon." Mary put her shoes back on and stood up. I put my shoes on too, then looked up at Mary. The sun was behind her head, and it hurt my eyes to see. In *The Abridged Picture Bible* the angel Gabriel makes a visit with the sun behind his head just like Mary. "You are Gabriel," I told her.

"You're loony." She grabbed my hand. We ran back to the wire fence and into school.

If you didn't tell Sack about a creek and a lip cut from a nose and two balls rolling and Mary's laugh and my song, were you telling a lie? I didn't know. I lay in my bed and looked up at the cracks in the shapes of wings. "Lord," I asked, "what is a lie? Is it if you don't tell?" The Lord said nothing; he only spoke to Sack.

The next night Sack went to bed early with her bad back. Sack's bad back sang her songs and told her stories of hope from the Bible when they lay together. I had to bring her white pills for pain and sleeping. Boot and me were downstairs. Boot was mixing boat glue in a little pot. The empty bottle was there, waiting. I lay on the floor with Cat. "Don't you want a pencil and paper, Hester?" Boot asked with a smile.

"No," I said. Paint at the school desk was better than a pencil at Boot's feet.

"But you like to draw your funny little things—why don't you want to?"

"No," I said. Cat jumped over my tum, and did a roll. I laughed the devil's language.

"What are you doing at that place?" Boot asked. Cat's tail tickled my nose. "What are you doing there?" I didn't know what Boot wanted me to say so I kept quiet as Boot's eyes traveled from my toes up over the rest of me.

That night I woke up, soft footsteps on the floor, my room a black blanket. "It's only me," said the whispering voice of Boot.

"Am I in trouble?" I asked.

"Hetty, shhhh," Boot said. He took quiet steps to my bed and then he sat on it, making me tip into the middle. He patted my head the way I pat Cat. I went to my bird dream but Boot pulled me back. He reached his warm hand under the blanket, "Shhhh." His hand was between a tickle and a smack. It moved faster; it got under my nightie and then Boot got in my bed. My bed made a *creak creak* noise. I laughed and then I didn't. "Don't cry, Hetty, shshshsh." Boot's hand sat on my mouth so my noises got stuck in between his fingers. He lay beside me filling up the whole bed. I closed my eyes as tight as I could so I got smaller and smaller until I was a tiny mouse in a hidey-hole. That way more room for Boot.

Boot pulled down his pajama pants like a man going to the toilet. Mouse went *squeak squeak*. "Don't cry, Hester, be a good girl." I lay as still as Lot's wife. Boot rolled on top of me. "*Creak creak*," said the bed. "Bad bed!" said Lot's wife. Down in the middle of the bed grew a strong tree, stronger than tree in the garden, stronger than street tree, stronger than school tree with the bench. Boot pushed the tree into Hester. His breathing was fast and his hand was on my mouth and a bit on my nose to catch all the noises.

The tree split my skin as its branches grew down my arms and legs. The branches grew out my fingers, out my ears and eyes, and burst out the top of my head. They spread over the bed and covered the ceiling so that all you could see was branches. The tree was cutting me in pieces like Sack cut the meat for dinner. Blood sprayed out where I'd been split. I made a noise big enough to get past Boot's fingers and then God the Bird in the ceiling held out his wing with a song underneath and said, "Hide." I left Boot with the tree and

Lot's wife and I went to God the Bird and hid in the song of his wing.

When I came back only the stinging was left in the bed and that took up as much of the room as Boot.

My walk down the stairs the next morning was slow and stiff. Splinters stuck under my skin from the night before. Sack was scrubbing at the bottom of the stairs. "Dirt is caught in the corners, if you look close. Come and help." She dipped her brush in the bucket. Hot water spilled over the edges. I got on my hands and knees and scrubbed beside her. I watched the dirt come out of the corners and go into my brush.

"Do you talk to boys at school, Hester? Do they look at you? Don't let a boy touch you. What do they tell you there?" Boot asked me while I chopped. He looked afraid of something. *Chop chop chop*, *yes yes yes*, *more more more*, sang axe. I could have said a boy didn't touch me but one called me *fatty boom-sticks* and Mary took my hand, but I kept quiet and let axe do the talking *chop chop chop*, *yes yes yes*, *more more more*.

At school I painted Mary's lip and nose. They joined the snake of water and took us all the way to the frog. My teacher said, "Would you like to give your painting a name?"

"*Angel Gabriel and the Oldest Song*," I said.

My teacher shook her head and smiled. "You're a mystery, Hester."

・　・　・

Mary and me stood under the shelter with all the others who we were not the same as and waited for the bus to come. Will came over to me and said, "Why are you so stupid?"

"Bugger off," said Mary.

"Well, Mary, you tell me, then, why is she so stupid?" Will looked behind him at the other boys. They were laughing.

"I said bugger off!" Mary spoke louder this time.

"Be polite and answer my question."

"I'm not answering your dumb question."

"Why, are you stupid too?"

"Fuck off!"

"Your dad's a piss head, *you* fuck off," Will said, coming closer to Mary.

Mary stepped in front of me and smacked him with her hand open across his cheek. Will fell back, his eyes and mouth wide. "Fuck off," she said, breathing hard through her nose. Her face was redder than when we were fruit bats hanging from the branch. Will rubbed his cheek. There was fresh water in his eyes; it sprang from the source of his shame. He stepped back. Two boys came close to me and Mary. They were from the big class. One pushed Mary from behind so that she fell onto the other one.

"Ooh, don't touch me, Mary, I don't want your germs, they'll turn my face funny!" A big boy pulled at his lip and pushed at his nose so his face was a twist. "Get away from me, funny face." He pushed her back to the other boy. Mary hit his chin. He hit her back, not too hard. If he wanted to he could have hit her harder. He was going to do that now.

Birds flew over our heads. There was a circle of children that I was not the same as around Mary and the big boys. They were like the company I kept in the hanging room. I was in the circle and I was above the circle with the birds as they flew away. Mary ran at the big boy, wrapped herself around his middle, and tried to push him over. He knocked her very hard onto the ground. The circle watched. I was part of the company that I kept. The birds called to each other across the sky *caw caw caw!*

"Fuck you, bastards!" shouted Mary. A drop of blood came out her nose. The birds were black spots in the faraway when I ran at the big boy and knocked his big head hard into the back of the bus shelter. I heard it hit. The bus shelter shook. The boy didn't get up. The bus came. I took Mary's hand and we went on. Nobody said *crazies* this time. We sat side by side without speaking. The blood dried dark around the edge of Mary's nose.

A rope you couldn't see grew from me to Mary. The pictures in my head of Mary ran down the rope like water down a pipe, and into her, and her pictures of me ran down the rope straight back and into me. The rope got tight and knotted around us. Mary said, "When you go home tonight, think of me. Choose what I'm doing and what I'm wearing and I'll think of you and do the same. Then tomorrow we can tell each other if we got it right."

• • •

It was dinner. "You're not eating enough. That school is ruining you. Tonight I cooked fish and I want you to eat," said Sack. The fish lay on his plate-bed with potato and cauli for his blanket. He came all the way from the sea where everything is salt and dark water. In *The Abridged Picture Bible* Jesus filled the sea with red fish. He taught everybody how to catch them and eat them but he forgot to tell the red fish how to get away. Jesus doesn't have the time to think of everything.

"Eat the eye," said Sack.

"No," squeaked Hester Mouse, who knew an eye was to see with.

"Eat the eye!" Sack said louder.

"No!" squeaked Mouse from the corner.

"You eat the eye! You eat the eye! You eat the eye! Eat eat *eat*!" Sack stuck her fork into the eye of the fish and out it came and behind it there was nothing but darkness. There, in the empty head of the fish, was the darkness of the world.

Sack held the eye close to mine—closer and closer until I was looking into the eye of the fish, my eye into fish eye, fish eye into my eye, until it was me and my eye on the end of the fork.

"No!" I screamed with my mouth wide open, more like a loud girl in a school than a mouse in a hidey-hole. My mouth wide open, Sack stuck the eye inside and put her hand tight over my mouth so no spitting. Down dropped the eye—down, down, down into the deep of Hester and I could see, I could see with the new eye. I could see the inside of Hester and all of the inside was the same salt and dark water as where the fish came from and all of it was tears from the eye of the fish.

It was lunch at school the next day. We were eating Mary's grapes. Grapes are green and almost round. You can put sixteen in your mouth at the same time; Mary counted. After she swallowed the sixteen grapes she asked me, "Hey! What did you think of last night?"

"You spoke to the frog."

"Wrong. Well, I didn't think of you. Last night that bastard hit me and mum." *That bastard* was her father. "He was drunk as a skunk. But I don't care because of you," said Mary. My knee was up and bent and Mary leaned over and kissed it, then drew a circle in the dust with her finger. "Why don't you know the things everybody knows?"

"Things like what?" I asked.

"Things like what a grape is."

"Thine, O Lord, is the greatness and the power, and the glory—"

"Let's try for seventeen grapes, the world record!" Mary said, and laughed as she stuffed in the fruits. Her lip twisted up with her nose and jumped and wiggled, and it made me laugh too.

I came to school with stinging under my skirt and splinters under my skin. "It's our secret," Boot told me. A secret can belong to one person or it can belong to two people. Mary and me had the creek and the frog. Boot and me had night visits, pencil and paper, and the drawings in the kitchen bin. I had my own one-person secrets: hidden paintings and my friends at One Cott Road. The stinging was a two-person secret that burned. It burned while me and Mary chased each other across the black flat, it burned while my teacher said, "Repeat the numbers," and it burned while she read us a story. The story was about a donkey who turned into stone because he made the wrong magic wish. The donkey was like Lot's wife—she made the wrong magic wish too, and so did I. That's why Boot took his night visit that left me with a sting.

"It is a story about the importance of family," said my teacher. "Everything the donkey needed was right there, at home." She closed the book. "Time for singing." My teacher pressed a box button like on the radio at One Cott Road, and the music played. It was not the same as Sack's music. There were bells. My teacher said, "Come on, Hester, join in with the rest of us, you know the words!" Mary sang loud beside me. I looked at her singing and watched my teacher. I could see her pink tongue and her teeth with some bits silver when she sang. "*I danced in the morning when the world was begun/ And I danced in the moon and the stars and the sun/ And I came down from heaven and I danced on the earth/ At Bethlehem I had my birth.*" "Come on, Hester, sing!" said my teacher. Everyone was singing. I looked around at all the open mouths, at the sound flying out, full with bells. I opened my mouth. "Come *on*!"

"*Dance then wherever you may be,*" I joined in. The whole room was one open mouth singing. I was part of it. "*I am the Lord of the Dance, said he/And I'll lead you all wherever you may be/And I'll lead you all in the dance said he.*" My teacher's smile was a bridge. The singing in the room trickled over my stinging places like cool milk.

At the end of every day Mary and me caught the bus. Every day I got off at the top of Cott Road where Sack waited in her gown with the gray roses and her arms folded. Mary waved at me from inside the bus until the bus turned a corner. Every time I looked back Mary was still waving. I didn't wave because Sack was pulling me down the street but the rope of pictures between Mary and me held tight until the next day when I saw her again.

Today I came into the kitchen and Sack was there with my paintings in her hands and her eyes on fire. The pink spider turned in quick circles, his three legs twisting and reaching. The kitchen was hotter than the day outside. "I went to your room and this is what I find! What else don't you tell me?" Sack looked at one picture and then another and then another. The pictures flew past my eyes and fell to the floor. The kitchen filled with voices. The spoons, the chairs, the table, the floor, the handle, the axe, the doors—all the wooden things spoke loudly at once. I couldn't hear what they were saying as Sack turned my pictures over and over, faster and faster. "You have been hiding things from me! You have secrets!" Sack opened the door of the red wood stove. All my friends were quiet. The only voice was mine. "No!"

Sack got down on her hands and knees and crawled under the table faster than a cockroach under the shadow of Boot's toe. She grabbed at the paintings that lay there, gathering them up and pushing them into the fire. That hungry fire ate my pictures until there was nothing left but burnt pieces floating upward. As they rose up, the burnt pieces turned into black birds that flew hard into the window, as if the window was not there, as if the black birds could escape and fly straight into the sun and beyond, into eternity. But the window was there and the black birds hit so hard they knocked themselves out and lay dead on the floor, leaving blood behind on the glass.

Mary shouted through the rope that tied us together, "Fuck you!" Sack smacked me hard across my cheek and pushed me through the door in the floor, into the hanging room. I sat on the top step and table told me a story from there. She told me about the Ace of Spades and Whiskey and the day Mary rode the scooter so fast with the dogs pulling that it lifted and flew to One Cott Road and when it got to One Cott Road it came down through the open window and I jumped on the back and we rode to eternity.

When Boot came home I got a hanging that went on longer than all of the others. I never knew how I got to be in my bed with the lamb and the lion looking down.

• • •

I did not go to school for three days. I stayed in bed and Sack brought me soup and chops with peas. My arms were very sore from the hanging, so she fed me with a spoon. She read me a story. Jesus had a friend but one day the friend said, "I don't know you. I have never seen you." Sack read the same story over and over. She showed me the picture of the friend saying, "I don't know you. I have never seen you." The friend looked sad. He wore a long dark hat that made a shadow. Jesus looked sad too. The company he kept nailed him to a wooden cross with a hammer. They gave him a crown but it was made of thorns that pricked him. The hammer and the cross were his only friends. The cross said to him, "It's all right, Jesus, God the Bird is on his way." Jesus didn't look as sad after that.

When I went back to school black birds watched me from all corners. They sat on the branches of the paper tree and pecked at my name on the leaf as it danced, they flew between the books on the shelves. One guarded the building blocks, another hopped across boxes of pencils and crayons. They kept their eyes on me. I stayed still as Lot's wife. My teacher put the wooden brush in my stiff hand. I sat and held it but it didn't speak to me. My fingers went loose around the brush so that it fell to one side.

"Come on, Hester, you like to paint," my teacher said. Black birds flew around the room. I watched them land on the heads of the other children, on the plates of shiny colored paint, on the white paper. They left painted claw marks across the paper. They looked at me with black eyes and black beaks and I didn't take the brush. My teacher said, "Suit yourself, then." I listened to the class putting numbers together, then taking them away. When the teacher asked for a number all the other children that I was not the same as answered at once, in one loud voice, *seven, twenty-one, eleven*. They all knew which number, even Mary, they all knew when to answer *eighty, fourteen, six*. I didn't know the numbers or the words or the answers. I was an aberration and I only knew to sit. After lunch my teacher said, "Time for singing." Everybody took their songbooks from their desks. I heard the desks open and I heard them close. There was laughing around me. Everybody knew the time to laugh, the time to open a desk. My teacher pressed the button on the radio box and everybody sang. "*Morning has broken, like the first morning* . . . Come on, Hester, please join in."

"*Praise for the singing, praise for the morning.*" Mary pushed my side. "Sing, silly, sing!" but there was no song in me. It was burning in the red wood stove with my paintings. My song was finished.

"*Like the first dewfall, on the first grass.*" Mary sang with her eyes on me. "*Praise with elation, praise every morning.*" I put my hands over my ears so I couldn't hear the morning break.

. . .

At lunchtime Mary said, "Come and see the frog, Hester. Today it will be there, I know it. Come and listen for the oldest song." There was a black bird on her head, its claws hidden in her hair. The black bird shook its beak at me. Mary said, "Say something." The black bird stood there watching. Mary held out a green apple. The bird blinked his eyes. He wanted the apple for himself. "Hester, have some apple." The bird's beak was sharp as a knife; when he moved his head the beak shone along the edge. "Hester? Are you still my friend?" Mary asked me. The shine of the bird's beak was hungry. "Hester, come to the creek with me today, the frog will be there, I promise." The frog would be green—the color of grass, the color of Mary's socks and skirt, the color of leaves. "Please, Hester, you're my friend, Hester . . ." The frog would jump higher than the roof of the school; he would say, *Come on, Mary, come on, Hester, come for a ride on my back*. A tear came out of Mary's eye and ran down to where her lip joined up with her nose. More black birds made circles high in the sky over our heads. *Caw caw caw!* The bird on Mary's head bent down and the rope of pictures running from me to Mary, Mary to me, he took in his beak like a worm, and he cut it in half and all the pictures fell onto the ground around our feet; pictures of running water, songs, scooters, dogs, bottles, and rainbows—and then the earth pulled those pictures under.

"I don't know you," I told Mary, then turned away from her and ran to the toilet block. I sat on the cold floor of the toilet. The flushing chain hung down from a box above. I climbed onto the round white circle of the bowl. The chain wasn't long enough for both arms so I tied it in a knot around my neck only. I heard my teacher calling, "Hester! Hester, where are you?" The bell rang. Black birds joined in with the bell. They were calling me out. *Caw caw caw!* My teacher called, "Hester! Hester!" and the birds called, *Caw caw caw!* until I didn't know what was bird and what was teacher.

I stepped off the white circle. The lid of the world lifted over my head and I saw eternity shining in colors I'd never seen before. Everybody was there: handle, spoon, pencil. The toilet door swung open. "Hester! Oh, no, Hester!" My teacher's face was a long black beak with white eyes on top. She lifted my kicking body and untied the chain. I screamed for Sack because Sack knew it was the devil and she knew the words of the prayer. I called for her waiting at home in bed with her bad back and her pain. If I called loud enough the sound would travel the roads that the bus took and it would reach her ears and it would go down from her ears and into her arms and legs and neck and then Sack would stand up and run to the school, faster than the bus, faster than Boot in his chariot, faster than the black birds flying in circles she would run, she would be praying the strong words of God, the *up* of her shoes would be hard on the road *tap tap tap*, her eyes would be hot, the pink spider would shine in the street, and through it Sack would see where I was and she would come for me and the birds would fly up to the land of the sun, to where the tree was reaching, where they would burn until they were as dead as my paintings.

I screamed and my teacher drove her beak into my eye. It sunk in deep to where the fish swam in the salt and then she pulled out her beak and put it in my ear, to where wood spoke to me, to where my song used to sing. She drove it deep in and out of my eyes and ears. More teachers came running into the toilet. Blood was on my face and the face of my teacher. The teachers pressed me down; one sat on my legs, one held my arms. Everyone had a beak and I could see my own face in the shine.

Sack never came. They locked me in the sick room. I lay on the bed and looked through the window. The sky was gray and filled with circling birds.

When I woke up Boot was standing over me. My teacher was behind him. I looked at her face over his shoulder; it had no beak, and the bridge for walking lay in pieces on the floor. You could see broken wood and the bent ends of nails. There were three line cuts down my teacher's cheek.

"I am very sorry," Boot said. "We were worried about her coming here, but we were not given a choice. I think it has been a mistake. This incident . . ." He shook his head. I sat up. "It's time to go home, Hester. Everything is going to be all right, but we must go home now." He took my hand and we walked out of the school. When I turned around my teacher was waving, her mouth made the word "Good-bye," then she turned and stepped over the scattered broken bridge to walk back into the classroom. I got into the back seat of the chariot and lay down so that I could see the sky as Boot drove. There was nothing there; no sun or cloud or rain or tree—the sky was empty.

I walked into the kitchen and Sack was there, sewing up holes. She jumped up from her chair. I let go of Boot's hand and Sack pulled me to her. Her bones went in me. She smelled like cat milk left in the bowl. "You don't belong there." She pressed her nose to my head. "Go to bed and I'll bring you soup and a bacon sandwich."

Boot and Sack took me for more tests. Sack wore a shirt with buttons the shape of Christ's heart that went all the way up to her neck, and a yellow skirt. Sack never wore a yellow skirt in One Cott Road. She wore her sleeping dress with gray roses. Her hair was up high and above her eyes was blue powder. The two rows of hairs around her eyes were thick black. There was brown powder almost the same color as her skin, over the top of the pink spider. He had to wave his legs to try and brush it away. Sack turned to me where I lay across the back seat. "You should never have gone there; you didn't belong. I told them that."

Boot said, "Everything will be all right." I looked up and saw the egg of his head bob up and down as he drove. "This time they will see." He scratched his shoulder as if he was giving it a punishment.

• • •

The tests were not with the man who gave me the pencil and told me to put the square into the circle; they were with a lady wearing a white coat. I looked at her shoes; they were squeezing her feet so tight that her feet were spilling over the edges.

"I am Doctor Reed," the lady said. Doctor Reed shook the hand of Boot. "Perhaps you should be in the room while we examine Hester. Would that make you more comfortable?" Sack shook her head for a *yes* and smiled for a *thank you*. Her yellow skirt was a candle. I had never seen Sack smile for a *thank you* before. In her eyes was the start of two fires. Those I had seen before.

Boot, Sack, and me followed Doctor Reed into the testing room. "We told the school that we didn't think it would work and I'm sorry we put Hester through it," said Boot, sitting down on a chair.

"I think Dr. Mellick was probably a little hasty in his decision, but he really wanted the best for Hester." Doctor Reed wrote notes. "He is well aware of how big a burden it is to have a child like Hester at home full-time. You have obviously been doing a very good job."

Sack did the *thank you* smile again. "She is my daughter. A daughter is never a burden."

"Help us!" called the feet of Doctor Reed. "We want to escape from Doctor Reed and go with you and Mary to the creek where the soap is made of dirt and where the frog is hiding." Doctor Reed's toes were trapped inside her tight shoes. They were being held prisoner the way Jesus was kept a prisoner the night before the crucifixion. I pointed at them. Boot pushed my hand back down into my lap. I could not free the toes of Doctor Reed.

She looked up from her note. "I am not a parent myself, so I cannot imagine. I can only admire your commitment."

"I think it helps that there are two of us," said Boot, from the other side.

"Of course. Now let's take a look at Hester." Doctor Reed looked into my ears and eyes with long glasses. She put me on a table and pressed my tum. She squeezed my arms and legs and made me bend them. Her hands were cool on me. In the corner of the room a single black bird watched.

"Hester is physically well enough. She's clearly been in some tussles at school. Perhaps some of the bruises were incurred during the incident on her last day. And we know what caused the marks on her neck. It says in my report that she had to be held down by three members of staff. But there's nothing serious here for you to worry about physically. It is difficult when a child's problems are mental rather than physical. We can't see them; we can only experience the evidence of them. I think that can be far more challenging. Parents often go without the support that they need in raising a child like that. And these disorders are far harder to diagnose. Modern medicine has come a long way, but we still have a long way to go. I am going to prescribe something for Hester that will help her to be calm, so that she does not have the mood swings that you described in the report forms."

"We love our daughter very much," said Boot. "It's an effort but we want her at home with us."

"How frequent are these violent outbursts when she is at home with you?"

"When Hester stays home we can keep her life very regular. We find that if things stay the same, without too much change, then Hester is manageable." Boot's egg hung on the side as he talked. He was trying hard to stop himself from scratching.

"The thing you must understand is that we cannot predict Hester's behavior in the future."

"We have always understood that," said Sack. Her skirt glowed bright as a candle for the dead.

"I think you're both very brave people," Doctor Reed said. "I believe that the best place for Hester is home with you, but that may change. There may come a time when Hester will have to go to a special care hospital. You need to know that is always an option. Hester may become more difficult as she grows into an adult."

The black bird swooped down onto Doctor Reed's head. It took a nibble on her ear. I took Sack's bone and held on tight. "We'll be home soon, Het," she said, with the new smile.

Doctor Reed stood up. "I've taken enough of your time. Take your daughter home, and please consider options for the future if it gets too much for you both."

"Don't go!" the doctor's feet called to me. This time they were crying.

Boot shook hands with Doctor Reed again. "Thank you, Doctor," he said. "I only wish that Hester had never had to go through any of this." The black bird put his beak in Doctor Reed's ear and pulled out a small worm. I tugged on Sack's bone. It was time to go.

"Thank you, Doctor Reed. We should get Hester home." Sack stood up from her chair.

"Of course. Good luck to you both." The bird swallowed the worm and gave me a wink.

In my bed of dark that night I closed my eyes and a picture of me and Mary came down the rope. It was a picture of the water in Mary's eye. The water grew into a tear and fell slowly from her eye, moving down her cheek until it joined where her nose mixed in with her mouth. I heard myself say, "I do not know you." I saw a picture of the hole that the doctor made in Mary for the air to come through. I saw a picture of six feet under. It was dark as the cave where Jesus hid. I saw Mary's kiss on my knee and the snake of water. I saw oranges, apples, and grapes. Juice jumped from our mouths.

A tear in my closed eye tickled my cheek as it ran down my face.

Every day I did my duties. Boot went to his work and at nights he shut himself in his study and Sack sat in her bed and sewed up holes. Sometimes Sack came downstairs but Boot and me never knew when. Whenever she did Boot made her tea and looked at her with wide eyes, hoping she might pat his head the way she patted the head of Cat.

I didn't draw pictures anymore; they drew me instead. I was the pencil, but whose hand was holding me? At night I was drawn into trees, leaves, and water. The water could not be held; it dripped, leaked, and dribbled. I was drawn into a lion. I looked for Jesus so I could sit at his royal feet and purr but I couldn't find him. He was visiting his mother in a town I had never been to.

I asked the wooden things, my old friends. I said, "What is happening?" But they kept quiet. They knew the answer but they didn't know when they would give it to me. The little hand went around and around, I couldn't count how many times. I was waiting, but for what? What did I think was coming? Day passed then night passed then day passed. What path did the days follow? Why were there so many? What were they for?

Sack told me I was going with her to my grandmother's. She told me she needed help, with the cleaning and the looking after. "Your grandmother is very sick, you mustn't upset her."

"What is a grandmother?" I asked Boot, later.

"The mother of your own mother," he answered. Grandmother was the mother of Sack. Everybody had a mother; they conceived you unless you were Jesus. He was not conceived.

He was a miracle. Sack was my mother though I was a curse, not a blessing. Was Sack a curse to her mother, or a blessing?

Sack wrapped a scarf around my neck, put on her coat, and said, "Time to go." When I stepped outside, the night hid what was close and showed me what was far away. I turned in a slow circle, my face turned up to the moon and the stars. I was made of a body but the inside of me spilled out past the body the way water spills out of a sponge when the sponge is too full. The inside of me reached up into the night sky and then it went beyond the night sky into eternity. "Hester, stop that. Walk with me." Sack stepped onto the street and I followed. Dogs barked as we passed. The air was cold on my face. Sack said, "Hurry." Sack was fast; her fingers with the needle, her arms in the bucket, her legs on the street; her stirring, sewing, spreading of the sheets over the bed. I was slow as worms on the grass looking for a hole. My feet made a walking song with Sack's. *Tap tap tap* (Sack). *Boom boom boom* (Hester). *Tap tap boom tap tap boom tap tap boom.* It was a long way; I got a hot neck under my scarf, and a hot wet face.

We came to a house at the end of a thin street. "We're here," said Sack, taking out her key. She unlocked the door and we went inside. We walked down a hall past a painting of a horse eating hay with his long head down. I followed Sack into a room. My grandmother sat in front of a fire that burned in a metal box. She was the color gray with a blanket on her knees. A white web of hair grew over her head. When my grandmother saw me she held out her arms. The blanket fell from her knees onto the floor and she said, "At last! At last!" Her eyes were like Sack's, but faded, as if they'd been hanging on the line in the sun too long.

"Don't make a fuss, it hasn't been possible before now," Sack said.

My grandmother took me in her arms and held me tight. "Call me Mog—it's what your mother called me when she was little. She called me Moggy before she called me Ma. My name will be our secret." Mog's whisper was a warm tickle on my skin. I had a new secret whose name was Mog. "Your mother isn't well . . . I'll teach you how to play checkers. Come sit on my knee, little Hester—not so little anymore." Very slow, very soft, she touched the blue circles on my arms and legs. "That father of yours." She shook her head. "Hopeless."

Sack stood with her hands on her hips in front of my grandmother's chair. "We have work to do."

Mog held me by the shoulders in front of her. "You made me wait so long. Why did you?"

"You haven't been well enough."

"Am I better now?"

"Now I need help to take care of you. That's why she is here."

Mog turned to me. "At last."

Sack was in the outside laundry soaking sheets. I was wiping the bench of Mog's kitchen with the cloth. She called me over. "Tell me everything, Hester, everything. I want to know, I don't have long." I looked around my grandmother's room for black birds. "Speak to me, Hester." I couldn't see any black birds. "Hester?" Somebody had drawn tiny pictures over my grandmother's face. I saw the flowers from the garden, the branches of the tree reaching up, and leaves on the vine around her eyes. I touched a leaf with my finger. My grandmother put a kiss on the end. "Talk to me. Tell me things."

"What?"

"Anything. I want to know."

"I don't know."

"Do you have friends?"

"Yes."

"Who, then?"

"A friend gives you pictures."

"You are right. That is what a friend does. Will you give me a picture?"

"Yes."

"I would like that. I will put it on the wall above my bed. It will be a way of having you when you are not here."

"Where will I be?"

"At home where you live."

"Why can't I live here?"

Mog smiled and touched my cheek. "I wish you could. Who are your friends, Hester?"

Who were my friends? Handle, table, chair, broom, axe, and Mary. "Mary," I said.

"Who is Mary?"

"My friend."

"Where did you meet her?"

"School."

"And what pictures did Mary give you?"

The rope that tied me to Mary tightened around my throat. "She ate the world record in grapes."

"Do you like school?"

"I don't go there now."

"Why not?"

"I am not the same as other children."

"You don't need to be."

"What is need?"

"I need you." Her hands were two cups on my cheeks.

I wanted to let my secrets out. I was overflowing with them; they had grown too big, been left alone too long. My secrets wanted to pour into the cups of her hands until her hands were full and she could drink the secrets from them like warm tea. "I hung upside down because I was a fruit bat. I held up the fence and it cut a line of blood. My name danced. It was a leaf. You can find a whole tree in every leaf. A donkey made a wish. That was before. After there were black birds in all the corners, on the heads and faces."

"What faces? Where?"

"Everywhere. They were in the corners but they wanted to come down, it was me they wanted, they were hungry for my words and my secrets that lived down deep where everything was salt from the tears of the fish. The black birds flew in circles—"

"What circles? I don't understand."

"Mary had one on her head; it wanted the apple. Mary said the apple was for me, she held it out, and the black bird watched. He was angry, he wanted the apple."

"What are you talking about? What apple?"

"I ran to the hanging room, the teacher came."

"I'm sorry."

"Her face was a beak."

"I'm sorry that—"

"He wanted my eyes—"

"I'm sorry that it has to be—"

"The black birds wanted to eat my eyes. They wanted to peck me *peck peck peck*!"

"Get my blanket. Where's my blanket?"

"*Peck peck peck!*"

"Where's my blanket?"

"*Peck peck peck!*"

"My blanket! I need my blanket!"

"It's on your knee."

"Where's my blanket? Get my blanket!" Mog shouted.

"On your knee. It's on your knee."

"Where is my blanket? I want my blanket! Get me my blanket!"

Sack came running. "I told you not to make trouble!" She took the blanket from off Mog's lap and wrapped it around her shoulders. "There it is, Mummy, there it is, can you feel it now?"

Mog stroked the silk edge of the blanket with her fingertips. "My blanket, I need my blanket, don't ever take it from me again."

"Nobody is taking your blanket, Mummy. Can you feel it there?"

"I can feel it, yes yes."

"Hester, you must leave your grandmother alone. She is very sick. Don't upset her, it doesn't matter what she says to you, leave her be and help me." I walked backward, away from my grandmother.

I helped Sack clean. We changed the sheets on Mog's bed. Beside the bed was a small cupboard with a light on top and a cross and a picture of a man standing beside a metal bird. I picked up the picture of the man. There were badges on his coat and big glasses on his head. He had Sack's eyes without the spider. I dusted the picture with the dusting cloth. "Be careful with that, Hester." Sack took the glass picture from my hands and looked at it. After a while she said, "Butter wouldn't melt in his mouth, would it?" She shook her head and kept staring at the picture. "Hero that he was."

"What did he do?" I asked Sack.

Sack stared at the picture as if I wasn't there and she was with the man beside the metal bird with badges on his coat instead. "He was my father."

"When was he?"

"A long, long time ago."

"What did he do?"

"He flew planes in the early days."

"What else?"

"He brought home the bacon."

"What more?"

"He wore a uniform."

"What else?"

"He was head of the house."

"Yes?"

"He took care of my mother."

"What else did he do?" Sack looked away from the picture and stared at the wall in front of her. The room was quiet. Every sound gone, there was only space and emptiness. "What else?" Sack waited. I waited. "What?"

"It was my twelfth birthday. Susannah from next door gave me a sun hat with a red ribbon. On the ribbon were five white baby ducklings following the mother duck. I wore the hat to bed that night." Her words filled the room the way water fills a bottle—slowly, from the bottom up. "My father said, 'You can take that off now.' I didn't want to take it off. He said, 'Take it off.' I said, *No, don't make me, please don't make me, please don't, don't make me, I don't want to, please don't make me! No no no!* 'Take it off,' he said. I didn't have a choice. If you don't have a choice it means there is only one thing that you can do, even if it is as bad as jumping in front of a moving train, or cutting yourself, or falling from somewhere very high—you still have to do it. Somebody else makes you. I took off the hat. I laid it on the floor by the bed. If I'd been lying under the bed beside it, my father's weight on the mattress would have pushed the mattress down so that it would have touched the tip of my nose. He was a big man. But I wasn't lying under the bed beside the hat; I was lying on the bed beside my father. There was nobody under the bed, only a dark space. There was nobody. *No, please don't, no, I don't want to, don't make me.* I said it but it made no difference." Sack had never told me such a long story; longer than a story from the Bible, and without pictures. I had to make the pictures for myself. When Sack looked up she seemed surprised that I was there. "I never counted another birthday after that. It was my last one. I didn't want any more." Her eyes were wide. She looked like she didn't know why there were clouds and streets, or why to pray, or why to live in a house with Boot or why she was a mother or why to eat and sleep and why to wash the curtains and why to wait at the bus stop or go to sleep at night. "He's dead, anyway," she said, after a full turn of the hands around the clock face. "You don't need to dust that one, you can just leave it." The man kept watching me with Sack's eyes from behind the glass.

When we finished the cleaning Sack helped my grandmother to bed. She dressed her in a pale pink gown and said, "I will be back tomorrow." When Sack wasn't looking I whispered in Mog's ear, "That father of yours . . . hopeless." Then I kissed her. It was soft as paper.

Sack took me to Mog on Sundays. It was always at night so I could help put her to bed. Mog asked questions and said my name, *"Hester."* She took my hand when Sack was in the kitchen making soup. She patted it the way I patted Cat. She said, "My little girl, I have had to wait so long. Why did I have to wait so long?" Then she screamed, "Get my blanket! Where's my blanket? Why do I have to be cold? You know how I hate the cold!" I never knew when she would scream; it was always a surprise.

Before I'd seen Mog, had she always been in her chair? What is *at last*? I made pictures of her dry hands tracing lines around the blue circles on my arms and legs. "Sit on my knee, your mother's upstairs, she can't see." She pulled me up and pressed my head against her chest. Sleep came, no God the Bird, only Mog, *pat pat patting* my head. I purred like Cat till Sack came and said, "Get off!"

Sometimes Mog called out, "The pain, the pain!"

"What is the pain?" I asked her.

"All over."

"Where is it from?"

"The mistakes I made and never fixed. I left it too late."

"What is late?"

"Help me."

"What is it?"

"In my body."

"Who put it there?"

"I don't know who put it there! God put it there. Oh, the pain!"

Sack came and prayed over her and put the holy water on her head and whispered in words I didn't know. At night I lay in bed and whispered, *The pain the pain!*

Mog had the sicks—*Her heart is missing*, Sack said. *Beat beat beat then nothing. It misses.* We did the walk in the day, first time. I had not been for a day walk since school finished. The sun in the sky was so bright that I had to cover my eyes with my hands. Orange lights jumped behind my fingers and spread into shapes of cats and worms and a puddle. I opened my fingers for a small look in between. Everything was lit up bright as the sun: gardens with colored flowers, trees full of silver and green leaves, the sky shining white and blue—lovely like my paintings and my song. Morning had broken. I started to cry. "The street is watching," said Sack, but I couldn't stop. The street watched as creeks of water fell from my eyes and I made sounds like Cat caught on the high gate. I could see past the land of the sun, past all things touchable and hard, into eternity. I saw the shadow of the wing of God the Bird, where he waited. I cried louder. Sack pinched the back of my neck and that is a good way to stop me crying but I didn't stop. I cried all the way to Mog's with Sack pulling me by my arm. When we got inside Sack said, "That's enough!" She went to fill the bucket and I walked into Mog's room, still sniffing.

She lay in her bed with her heart missing. If there was a hole in her nightdress the same as the hole in Christ's, there'd be no red heart with the green thorns wrapped around, only a dark space showing the parts you couldn't put a finger on. Mog's eyes were shut. I went very close and looked at the tiny drawings on her face. A boat sailed along the small sea of her forehead. She opened one eye, then closed it again. "Mog," I said. She didn't say my name and she didn't touch the blue circles on my arms. Sack made her soup with a carrot, ham, and an onion floating, and I cleaned her floors and her wall. When Sack wasn't looking I took her hand. It was like holding a shoe or a stick with no grandmother in it at all. "Mog," I whispered into her paper ear. "At last, at last."

She opened her eyes and said, "I never stopped him, he was my husband; I didn't stop him." She reached up and touched my hair. "My little one, so perfect." She called for Sack: "Kathy!" Sack came close and my grandmother said, "I should have stopped him, all those years. Why didn't I stop him?" Then she tried to suck a ball of air into the deepest parts of herself. I heard the ball of air fighting with my grandmother. It didn't want to go in, it wanted to stay on the outside where there were no walls of grandmother skin telling the air when to stop. The ball hit the insides of my grandmother as she tried to drag it in. It bounced around the walls inside her as they fought. But it was my grandmother who needed the air; the air didn't need my grandmother. Only I did. Sack kept saying, *"Mummy, don't don't,"* as the pink spider wriggled and spun. Tears ran down his spider cheeks. I saw the ball of air fly out of my grandmother and she went still. She was empty like the skin of a sausage with no sausage inside. She went flat. Sack fell over her and coughed and coughed and held on. As I watched Sack grew smaller until she was so little she fit under my grandmother's flat empty arm. She went under it and she cried. Soon she turned around to me, eyes red at the edges, pink spider covering his small hairy face, and said, "Leave me here for a while. You go out and fold up your grandmother's things. I won't be long." But she was long. She was as long as a day. I folded Mog's blanket then I unfolded it. I folded it again, then sat in my grandmother's chair, spread the blanket over my knees, and slept.

When I woke up the room was in darkness. Mog's blanket had fallen from my knees and I was cold. I sat up. Mog swam in water around my head. She had no body, only an invisible heart. She was leaving the room. I followed her down the hall, then she opened the front door. She said, "Everything will be all right," then she flew up into the sky and her invisible heart joined with the stars so there was one extra. God's peace was in me; it made me soft. I walked back into the house, sat in Mog's chair, and fell asleep.

When Sack came out and woke me up she was her old size again. It was dark when we walked back to One Cott Road. This time our feet were very quiet. Silent eternity was above me as Sack pulled me along with her head down.

The next day, after porridge, I said, "Where has my grandmother gone?"

Boot touched Sack on her shoulder. "Quiet, Hester," he said.

The question in me pushed up along the wet walls of my throat. It wouldn't be stopped. "Where did she go?"

Sack sniffed, her hands in the sink washing porridge pot.

"Quiet, Hester," said Boot.

"Where?"

"Gone to God." Sack turned around to me. Her hands dripped with sink water. The pink spider nodded at me.

My question bumped and pushed. "But—but *where*?"

"To the cemetery," said Sack with tears running through.

"Where is the cemetery?"

"My mother . . ." said Sack with her head in her hands. Boot took her upstairs, shaking his head at me as they went.

I sat with Cat under the kitchen table when Sack was in the church. I told Cat about Mog and the cemetery. I tickled under her black and gray chin. "A grandmother is the mother of your mother. You are conceived. She said she never stopped him and he was her husband. There was a picture of a man and he was Sack's father, he flew planes in the early days and she said, *No no no please don't please.* My grandmother was on her way to the cemetery. Does she have her blanket there? *Catty Catty Catty.*" Cat purred but she didn't answer. Nobody did.

As the hands of the clock turned circles I waited for pictures from my grandmother. They came to me at night. She touched my bruises and she wrapped her blanket around me and said, *At last at last.*

One day I woke up with sticky slow dripping from between my legs. I put in a finger and it came out red on the end. I pulled back the blankets and a blood flower grew on the white sheet. There were two blood flowers on my white nightdress too. I traced the petals with a finger. They were like the flowers in the Garden of Eden before Adam listened to what Eve said. Two tight fists wrung out a damp red cloth in my tum. I rolled over with my hands to warm me up. The fists wrung the cloth again. I heard Sack downstairs singing *Jesus Jesus*, while she stirred the pot. If she found the flowers there'd be trouble. Jesus beat the drums from the feasts in my chest *beat beat beat*. I pulled off the sheets and the nightdress with hot in my face and the two fists wringing in my hungry place. I should be downstairs setting the table.

"Hester?" Sack's voice came up the stairs.

The drum beat faster *beat beat beat*. Sheets in my hands, I looked around the room but I already knew all the corners and there were none for hiding. I was very hot in my face and the fists wrung the red cloth again, tighter this time; I needed the toilet.

"Hester!" I heard her feet on the stairs—Sack hated the stairs, her back needed lie-downs and day-sleeps, not stairs. The hot in my face turned cold and the fists pulled the cloth so tight I had to sit down. I needed the toilet more, *more*. Sack was halfway up the stairs. I wanted to say, "Stop! Sack, stop!" I wanted to run down the stairs, push past her to the toilet, and let my bottom end have a rest. "Hester, what are you doing?" She was at the top now and then she opened the door, walked into my room, and looked at me with eyes like streetlamps—I was the street. The two fists squeezed the cloth tighter and tighter, red water dripped out, my bottom end opened up, and it was too late for the toilet. "Hester! How could you?" She grabbed me around the back of my neck with her thin hand and pushed me to the stairs. "Go outside and wash yourself. Filthy!"

I was filthy and my filthy swine sounds filled the room. I ran hard at Sack and her back hit the wall with her breath jumping out like a punch. She fell to the floor with the sound of a dropped cup and then I sat on her with the blood flower sheets over her mouth and my filthy swine smells all around us. Sack hit the air with her hands and she pushed me off. The pink spider shook his angry leg at me. Sack backed out the door.

It was nighttime. I lay awake with the fists wringing out the cloth when Boot stepped softly into my room. "It's me," he said. Me climbed in and God the Bird swooped down from a cloud and stretched out his wing for Hester to climb on. I was halfway up when Boot fast-jumped out of the bed. He was leaving the room, his breathing fast and frightened. God the Bird flapped his wings and flew away. Sticky trickled between my legs. I got up out of bed and switched on the Christ light by the door; there were more blood flowers on the sheet.

Boot never made another night visit. In the kitchen his eyes looked at the plates and the pots, the spoon stirring around, and never at me. I was not his good girl anymore. Sack found every flower and we prayed together. She ripped up sheets and tied them in pieces around me.

The hands went around and around the face on the kitchen wall; I counted up to seven, then started at the front again. There were too many circles to fit in a single day. There were too many days. One started; light behind the curtains, birdsong, the light grew brighter, it stretched and rose and shone, birdsong quieted, then light sank slowly into bed. I watched the day pass, I counted it passing, as it darkened and became night. I watched that pass too, on my back looking up. Darkness spread out over the world, grew thick, lit only by the moon, then it slowly thinned, turning to gray, until the darkness passed, and another day began. I never knew where the day had gone. I didn't know how I could get any of them back. Where do you look for a lost day? As the hands went around the face of the kitchen clock, my body grew pieces like the hills Christ walked over with his basket of bread and cheese. Sack saw me looking. "No!" she said. I didn't look after that, but I touched. The hills felt soft and they tickled. Hair came out of me like spider legs. "Where are the spiders?" I asked Sack. "Under your skin," she told me. "It is what happens to women."

I was cleaning the toilet on my knees on the hard floor. It was my duty. When I went to put my brush in the bucket of water I saw a face. When I dipped the brush in the bucket the face spread and broke into pieces—the pieces swimming away from each other as if they were enemies.

I looked in the mirror that hung in Sack's room. She caught me doing it. "What are you looking for?" I looked in the mirror to see a new person in the house—*a young woman of eighteen*, Boot told me.

"What is eighteen?" I asked him.

"Eighteen years since the day you were born," he said.

"Is that a long time ago?"

Boot stopped his reading and looked up at me. "No, it's not long, no." I looked in the mirror to see what was not long ago. I looked to see what Cat liked to scratch and sit on, what Sack liked to pray beside, what Boot liked to lie on before the flowers of blood. I looked in the mirror to see an aberration.

•   •   •

The same river of blood that flowed through Christ and the townsfolk caught in the tower of Babel flowed through me. It swelled big as the sea after the storm, the one that set Noah on the boat. The river pushed at its own banks as it flowed and itched the way Boot itched when he had his eczema. Sack said, "Stop scratching at it, John, you know it will only get worse." She painted pink medicine wings across his shoulders—but he still scratched when she wasn't looking. The river of blood wanted to burst out of my open mouth. Sack stayed farther back from me, as if she knew the river inside me was flowing so hard and fast she might drown in it.

I lay in my bed and heard someone else in trouble—not me, not Cat, but Boot. "Everything you do is wrong!" Sack couldn't put Boot in the hanging room; he was too big to get up onto the table. She could only shout.

"Katherine, please don't say these things." A heavy pot hit the floor. The river of blood inside me flowed faster when I heard that pot hit the floor. I grew bigger than the bed. My arms and legs hung over. I filled up the room. The river of blood wanted to spray from the wide holes of my new big self. I got out of the bed; my door was locked. "Open! Open! Open!" I called. Nobody came but One Cott Road went quiet. No more Sack shouting, no more pots hitting the floor.

In the morning Sack took a long time to come and open my door. I had made a puddle in the corner. Sack said, "You're not a little girl anymore. You're a young woman. Surely you can hold on." She laughed the laugh of a little bird whose beak is too small to let out the sound. Jesus beat the drum from the feasts faster inside me and the river of blood flowed strong and wide. *Whap!* I hit Sack where the beak would be if she was a bird. She fell over and both her wings went *snap!* Her hair lay in my puddle and I came for her again. All the years of my eating landed on the back of Sack. "How long will ye vex my soul?" I asked her.

"John! John!" she called, her words catching in my fingers over her mouth, the way mine caught in Boot's. Boot came running up the stairs and into the room. "Hester, no!" He tried to pull me off Sack but you can't stop a river of blood flowing wild by saying *no*. I hit him where his tree grew, then I hit him again, in the nose. He threw me at the wall—the wall caught me and threw me back. I hit him again and again, in his eyes. Then he gave me one more big push and that wall knocked me on the head and said, "Sleep time." When I woke up the room was empty. I was lying in a pile by the wall with a sore leg and a sore elbow and a sore head.

For days and days they left me alone. No punishments, no duties, no Bible lessons. I stayed in my room and drew pictures with my fingers over the walls. The pictures were all secret ones—you couldn't see them. Cat could but Cat would never tell. I drew the river of blood; One Cott Road was in it, bobbing up and down, more down then up. I drew me standing on the edge of the blood river with a long stick. I pushed

One Cott Road under with the stick so you could only see the chimney and then I pushed that under too.

Boot let me out to go to the toilet and brought me food. One day I listened at the door. It was Boot saying, "We can't do it anymore. We don't have the strength."

Sack said, "But she is my daughter."

"You aren't well enough, Kathy. We don't have a choice. Look what she did to you. What will happen next?"

Boot came into my room. "Hester, you're going to live in a new place."

I was drawing a lamb and a snake on the floor. The snake was swallowing the lamb in one bite. "What place?" I asked him while I finished with the lamb; the last thing to go down was his wriggling tail.

"Renton."

"What is Renton?" I asked, looking up at Boot.

"Renton will be your new home."

"Why will it be?"

"We can't take care of you anymore."

"What is taking care?"

"You will be taken care of at Renton."

"Where will you be?"

"Here."

"Where will I be?"

"Renton."

"Will Cat be there?"

"Cat will be staying here." Boot's turn to sit on the bed. Would he take my hand, would he say my name again? Would it be full with the tears from the eye of the fish?

"Hester—I am—I am . . ."

"What are you?" I asked.

"We never should have, I never should have . . ." His hands made a cover for his crying eyes.

"Where will you be?"

"I don't know. I don't know where." His hands came down from his eyes. I looked into them; they were brown with red tears. There were lines down his face that went from the sides of his nose to the corners of his mouth. Whose knife had made those lines? Whose hand held the handle?

Sack's body in my room made the room smaller, pressing me to the walls. Sack fast-opened cupboards, fast-pulled-out clothes, fast-breathing as she prayed. Cat looked around the corner of the doorway. She walked slowly into the room with her tail up high. Cat knew she shouldn't come in. Sack saw her. "*Hisssssssssss*," she said, and out went Cat.

"We can't keep you anymore, Hester." As she spoke Sack folded the clothes and put them into a brown case. "You are— you are—a thief is what you are!" Then the talking stopped and she sat on the edge of the bed. Her white plaster arm looked hard as a door that wouldn't open. "Come here." She patted the place beside her on the bed. I came over and she took my hand. "Look at me, Hester." I looked in the blue water of her eyes. The pink spider held out a leg for me to hold. Sack said, "Hester." Her voice was full of tears from the eye of the fish. She held my hand in one of hers; all the knuckles on her fingers turned white as she held on. "Hester, when you were born, you came from *me*. It was the only thing I ever did that was right. You came from some part I couldn't see, or understand, I only knew that it was the best part." Sack touched the hair on the front of my head soft and slow. She moved my hair back from where it hung across my eye so I could see her whole.

I knew she would let go of my hand soon. I waited for it. She threw my hand away like she threw Cat out the back door. "You have to go, that's all there is to it." She stood up and left the room.

Once she was gone I came back from the edges and looked at the brown suitcase and the pile of my clothes inside it. On top of the clothes was *The Abridged Picture Bible* and on top of that was a painting that I did a long time ago when I went to school. It was a painting of me holding Cat. I wore a pink skirt. Mary was there, waving, and she had a halo. I didn't know Sack had kept that painting.

"It is time for us to leave." Boot stood in the hallway with the suitcase. Sack came past and opened the front door. She leaned more on one side than the other. She had a hand on her back and one in the white plaster and she was as thin as the stick that pushed One Cott Road under. Boot opened the back door of the chariot and I climbed in and lay down. I was much bigger now; I had to bend my legs to fit across the seat. Where was I going? Was it like school? Would Mary be there? Would my teacher be there? Would there be stories that traveled from the page and into my fingers?

We drove a long time before we stopped and Boot said, "This is it." We got out of the car and walked up a pathway with flowers on the sides. The flowers were orange with black eyes. I wanted to put my eye close to the black eye of the flower and see down to what lay hidden under the ground, but Boot was pulling; I had to keep up. We walked inside the building. It was not a house, not a school, and not the testing room. It was a new building. A lady came to us, with hair made of metal. Metal is what knives are, and forks. She held out her hand; it had three rings, one with sharp glass, and she said, "I am Dr. Pebblinghaus. Welcome, Mr. and Mrs. Wakefield."

"This is Hester," said Boot. Sack was crying. It made her cry, that I was Hester.

"I'm sure we can make the transition to Renton a smooth one for your daughter," said Pebblinghaus. She nodded at a lady wearing blue shoes. The lady took my arm. She was as strong as Boot.

Boot and Sack walked away. I called for them but they kept walking. Sack leaned on Boot. Boot leaned on Sack. Their bodies made an arch like the window on the cover of *Illustrated Hymns*. Through the window between them I saw the road leading away from me.

The lady with the blue shoes said, "This way." I followed her the way Cat followed Sack when Sack carried the meat. A man and a lady walked behind me wearing white shirts and the same blue shoes. The blue shoes made them light as the sky and fast. We walked along on a shining floor past many doors. I put my feet down slowly so that I wouldn't slip on the shining floor. Every door had a small square cut out and bars stuck in the square. We came to an open door. Inside was an empty room with a bed. The lady locked the door of the room with me inside and I made my smooth transition.

Hot light poured out over me from one bright ball. I looked around at the white walls without windows and at the ceiling without cracks. There was no corner dark enough for a secret, no shadow to hide a flat pencil. There were no friends hanging down, there was not the smell of meat, no cupboard for Cat, shoe, and coat—just me in the middle on my green sheet bed. The river of blood flowed faster. I itched like Boot, across the back and in all the holes. Moses and the reeds sunk down in the fast-flowing river. Pharaoh's daughter didn't find him in time. Nobody was here but me. I opened my mouth to call out so that my sound might be in the room too but all that came out were black feathers. I was choking on the feathers. They stuck in my throat. I coughed and the feathers flew in my face, catching in my nose and eyes. I threw myself at the door. The wall threw me back so I did it again, over and over. Two blue shoes came in. I held onto them. One gave me pills like Sack's for the pain. After they had gone the room turned into cloud. Jesus lived there; his chair was made of cloud and so were his dress and his hair. "Jesus?" I said.

"Yes?"

"Where are you?"

"In eternity."

"Have you forsaken me?" Jesus didn't answer because he was asleep—I heard him snoring in the cloud chair.

I made a picture of the face of the clock in the kitchen at One Cott Road and I tried to count the hands going around but the fingers on the hands going around grabbed hold of the numbers and threw them up in the air, changing the order so I couldn't tell what was an hour and what was a day. Was it one night that passed, or six? Was it eighteen years or an hour? A blue shoes opened my door. "Up time," he said, and I followed him across the shining floors into a big room. He told me to sit on a chair made of shiny green with a lot of ladies, all of them backs against the wall. Some ladies were big, some small. They wore green suits, the pants the same as the top. It was the same thing I was wearing. Who had given me these clothes? Where were *The Abridged Picture Bible* and my shoes? Some of the ladies looked at me and some didn't. None of them was Cat, Sack, Boot, or my teacher. None of them had seen One Cott Road, or my grandmother, or Mary. A small fire on the end of a white stick burned between the lips of every mouth in the room. The mouths sucked at the white sticks *suck suck suck*. I watched as smoke curled slowly up from all the nose-holes, making one big gray smoke cloud near the ceiling. We sat and we sat and the cloud became bigger and harder to see through. Sometimes the ladies spoke little voices into the smoke, where friends you couldn't see might live. One lady without any hair said, "Love my tits, don't you, Don! Love my tits, don't you, Don!" She said it over and over to Don, who lived in the cloud, and then she laughed as if Don tickled her. Soon a blue shoes said, "Dining room for breakfast." We stood up and walked into a room with long tables. Everybody sat around the table and I did too. The blue shoes wheeled in trays on a trolley that squeaked like mice. There were bowls of porridge on the trays and small piles of soft egg and a cup of tea in an orange cup.

A lady with two hard points and a long zip in between said to me, "I am Nurse Clegg. Do as I say and we will get along." She poured pink water into all the teas. "Drink up, please."

I put the spoon into the egg, and then I put the egg in my mouth. It sat there in my mouth, warm and soft. It wouldn't move. It didn't want to go down the dark hole, away from the sound and the light. I tried to swallow but my throat pushed up, not down. The egg landed on the table beside my plate. Nobody saw. "Go down," I whispered, before I put the egg back into my mouth. It sat trembling behind my teeth.

"Help me," cried the egg. My throat pushed up again and the egg landed on the floor. I got off my chair and went down there. I found the egg, still shaking.

"Go down," I whispered before putting it back in my mouth. Somebody kicked me and something warm trickled down my neck. It was tea and egg. A lady the color black said, "Eat mine too," and dropped her egg onto the floor beside me. I put more and more of the egg from the floor into my mouth where it sat trembling until a blue shoes put the tea to my lip and I drank.

The black birds came back. Their beaks turned into needles; the needles pushed through the skin and touched the hard bone. I woke in a tangle of straps. Water dripped down from my eyes *drip drip drip*, making puddles on the floor. It tickled as it fell. When I tried to smile I couldn't move my mouth.

What is it? I lifted my head high and looked. It was a box with little people inside doing tricks. "Television," said Nurse Clegg. "Watch it."

"Do the people locked inside the box ever leave?" I asked a lady sucking her thumb.

"Nup," she said.

"Not fair, is it, love?" said a lady knitting with no wool.

The people inside the television moved and jumped and changed color. I saw Jesus climb down off the cross. He told me to buy a silver chariot and drive it into a place with no trees or water. I saw dogs eating inside a white house with floors made of stone. I wanted to put what they were eating into my mouth. I saw a man with no clothes on. Water fell on his head and he sang, "*Come along! Come along!*" but I knew not to, because of the boasting.

I sat in the room that was mine trying to remember words to a prayer. *And the day of the Lord—and the Lord's day—like a thief in the night—the Lord's day, like a thief—the day of the Lord—the Lord's day, like a thief in the night—He will come—He will be—like a thief . . .* I couldn't close my mouth. Black birds flew in and made a nest of small sticks. I heard them *caw caw caw.* The sticks made tiny holes in the roof of my mouth. The black birds put their beaks in the holes and took small drinks of sticky red. The birds took up all the room in my mouth and then they pushed down into the deep places that you couldn't put a finger on. They pecked at the fish swimming there—catching them by the tail, throwing them up in the air, watching them glitter in the light above the water, then swallowing them like pills.

"Air time," said Nurse Clegg. Ladies made a line and Nurse Clegg said, "Out!" We breathed the air in the black yard with high wire all around. Some ladies stood at the wire and held on—they wanted to breathe the air that came from the other side. The other side was green with trees and a road. I wondered if a snake of water flowed down there, and if there was a frog. Some ladies talked to the air as they walked; they waved their arms and called out to friends I couldn't see. One said, "You're a genius, Marty, a real genius!" Another said, "It's a picture of me and my lost love, don't I look lovely?" And one said, "You can't poison me, not without a fight, you can't!"

I stood on the hard black ground as it spun in a circle around me. I got down on my knees and held on with my hands on the flat as it spun faster and faster underneath me. Porridge pushed up from my feet, past my throat, tongue, and teeth, until it sprayed out onto the hard black ground. With my hands in the hot wet I looked up to where God the Bird lived. *When will you come?* But God the Bird did not come to Renton; Renton was too far away.

It was breakfast again. Nurse Clegg went around the teas and poured in the pink water. "Drink up," she said. Every time she leaned her two points went close to a waiting face. If you turned your face the points would poke you in the eye. Nobody turned. Nurse Clegg poured the pink water into my cup. I picked it up and put it to my mouth. The cup was touching my lips when I heard a soft voice. "You don't have to drink it." I sat holding the cup to my lips. "You don't have to drink it. You can switch it. Watch." I watched. The lady who spoke to me pushed her cup across to another lady sitting with her eyes closed as if she was already sleeping. Then she took the sleeping lady's empty cup so that now it was hers. "See?" she said. My cup was still touching my lips. The steam from the tea went up my nose. This tea was not the same as the tea I made for Sack in One Cott Road; the pink water made it like something you wash the floor with. The ladies at the long table all drank their teas. "You don't have to drink it. It sends you straight to the Land of Nod with your eyes open," the lady said, looking at me. I looked back into the green eyes of Mary. She didn't have a lip twisted up with a nose, but it was Mary.

I put down the tea. "Mary," I said.

"What?"

"Mary."

"Who's Mary?"

"You."

"No, I'm not."

"Mary."

"I'm not Mary."

But she was. "Mary."

"I'm not Mary. I'm Norma K."

Her voice was the voice of Mary; it came from the mouth of Mary. "Mary."

"I'm not Mary, I'm Norma K. K is for Kyte, but you don't fly it. It's my name. K-Y-T-E, with Norma in front." She spelled it out the way my teacher did when I went to school. *A-P-P-L-E. Apple.* "Who's Mary?" she asked.

"You're Mary."

"You're nuts. Don't drink the tea unless you want to sleep all day with your eyes open."

Nurse Clegg said, "Time for the game room."

"Game room without the games." Mary-who-said-she-was-Norma smiled and winked. There was a dark gap on the side where her teeth were missing. I wanted to put my eye to the gap, see what secret was hiding in there. The points of

Nurse Clegg were close to my face. "Drink up, please." Mary snorted and I drank the pink tea.

A man in the television told us to dig the earth and watch for weeds. A weed is unwanted and takes over. You can't stop it, even if that is your wish. The weed grows and grows unless you dig it out at its deepest part, at the part that joins it to the earth, at the root. If you dig it out at the root with your spade, pulling up the branches, some as fine as hairs, if you pull up every one, then the weed will die in your hand. If it dies in your hand then it lives some other life in an invisible land for dead things that doesn't matter to you because you've never been there so you can't make pictures of it because what would you put in those pictures? You don't know anything about that land full with unwanted weeds, but if you leave even the finest hair of a root in the earth then the living weed will grow its plant back again and take over. You have to dig deep; you have to take it all. I watched Mary from across the room. She was looking for something, I didn't know what. She turned her head from side to side, she tapped the seat, and her legs jumped up and down. Did you see the frog, Mary? Did you make pictures of me even after the black bird bit the rope in half? Did the bastard hit you?

Mary-who-said-she-was-Norma sat beside me at dinner. Nurse Clegg walked around us with dinners on a trolley. There were peas, mash, and a sausage with brown. "Why are you always looking at me?" Mary asked.

"Mary," I said. Did the frog come? Did you ride on its back? As the hands turned slow circles around the face of the kitchen clock, when I bled flowers on the sheets and hung beside the company I kept, were you out riding on the back of the frog singing "Morning Has Broken"?

Mary slammed her hand down onto mine. "I'm not Mary. I'm Norma K. *K* is for *Kyte*. If you don't want the K, don't have it, but I'm not Mary. I'm Norma. N-O-R-M-A."

"Mary."

"*Norma*." She pinched the skin of my arm. "Say *Norma*." Her mouth made the slow shape of Norma. "Say it, or I'll pinch harder." If I said *Norma*, then where was Mary? "Say it!" The pinch was going to take the skin off. "Say it!"

"Norma."

Mary let go. "And never forget it." She looked down at the red star left behind on my arm. She touched it softly. "Sorry," she said. Mary was hidden inside Norma's skin. It was my secret. I said Norma, but I found Mary. I ate peas, mash, and sausage without sound because I wanted to hear the breath of Mary beside me *in out in out*.

At night, in my black room with the square cut out of the door, I drew the hanging room. Light from a candle showed me my friends hanging down around me. I wanted to be closer to them but it was hard to be closer when I was hung like a coat by my arms. I tried talking to them, *good morning good night good afternoon*, but they stayed quiet. I drew the stairs leading up, the darkness on the walls, and the eyes of Boot as he breathed faster and faster above me. I drew Sack on her knees, I drew Boot watching Hester at the woodpile, axe flying, *up down up down*. I drew the fires in Sack's eyes, her fast shoes, one in my throat. I drew all this with my eyes closed because when I opened my eyes black birds came flapping *peck peck peck*. I covered my eyes with my hands but the birds came *peck peck peck* at the cracks between my fingers. I shouted, "No!" Then the birds flew into my open mouth. A pair of blue shoes came into the room and put a needle in my bone.

I looked for the hanging room in Renton. "Where is under?" I asked Nurse Clegg. Nurse Clegg didn't stop to listen.

"Up your bum," said the woman the color black.

"Why are you that color?" I asked her.

"They shot me full of formaldehyde," she said, "so hot the needle melted and now I'm black." She laughed and I saw black inside. I drew the hanging room with my eyes closed and stayed there until it was time for the trays of food and the television again.

Blue shoes took us along the halls to the bathrooms. It was a row of taps, no bath. Blue shoes did the scrubbing with the hard brush and the soap. Some ladies cried and said *no*, but I stood still as Lot's wife as blue shoes ran the hard brush over my legs and back. I'd been washed before. Norma was under the tap beside me; she called to me through the water. "We're in a forest and it's raining on our heads."

"What is a forest?"

"In a forest there's only trees and nothing else. Maybe birds in the branches, and foxes, but that's it. You and me would be the only people," she shouted above the noise of the scrubbing and ladies crying *no*. We stood in the rain. All around us were dark trees. A blue bird with a golden throat flew in and out of the branches and a fox popped her red head through a hole.

The television was on. Some ladies watched, some slept, and some talked to friends who lived in the cloud of smoke near the ceiling. One said, "No way, no way in hell." Another said, "In all my life I've never!" Norma held out a white stick to me. "You want a fag?" It wasn't an orange. You couldn't eat it. "Go on, take it." I looked at the white stick. "Don't tell me you don't smoke?" I sat quiet. "Come on, I'll show you. Put it in your mouth." Norma put a white stick into my mouth and one in hers. Then she struck a match against the box. Her cheek flickered gold. She put the flame to the white stick in my mouth. "Suck it so it lights." I sucked for Norma and the white stick glowed with a small fire. "Suck harder." Norma laughed. Was it the devil? I sucked harder and the smoke from the white stick curled its way down to where the fish swam in the dark and quiet water. It brought God's peace to the places you couldn't put a finger on.

"You can let it out now." Norma smiled so that I saw the black gap in the side of her mouth. I let out the smoke and it burned and made me cough. Burning water filled my eyes. I sucked more. "You're a fast learner," said Norma. She lit her own white stick and we sucked in the smoke together. I coughed and Norma nodded her head and said, "Good job, good job."

Boot taught me the time. It was his lesson. *Small hand on one, big hand on twelve is one o'clock; small hand on two, big hand on twelve is two o'clock; small hand on three, big hand on twelve is three o'clock. That is time*, said Boot. *It ticks.* He held the clock to my ear and I heard a cockroach marching in circles *tick tick tick*. I watched the clock on the wall at Renton. It was the same one as home. Time was ticking there too.

"Airing Court, please," said Nurse Clegg. Her two points told us the way. Ladies walked in a line and out. "If you're going to be sick again, Hester, go and stand near the wire at the back."

The Airing Court turned in circles beneath me. I walked slowly to the wire. I wanted to get on my knees and crawl but blue shoes said no. The circle turned faster. Egg and onion was on its way. I bent over. Egg and onion was coming. Feet stood in front of me. I followed the feet up to find they were the long legs of Norma. "Walk with the same steps as me," she said.

Egg and onion waited. "Come on." Norma held out her hand. She had a picture of a butterfly there, drawn with a green pencil. "Come on, slowpoke!" I took her hand. The butterfly fluttered against my palm. She pulled me so I stood straight. "Don't you remember doing this at school?" She pressed her foot against mine so one foot was two. "Imagine our feet are tied together. Now walk." We walked, slowly at first, then faster. *One two, one two*, counted Norma. "If there was a race we'd win!" We walked around the edges of the Airing Court and the egg and onion stayed where it was.

We stopped at the wire and held on with our fingers. "Look out there, Hester. Do you want to go out there?" It was the green world, and the road leading away. "Well, do you?"

After a long time of nobody talking, only the quiet green world outside the wire waving its leaves at us, I said, "I want to hear the frog sing the oldest song." A black bird flew over our heads. He was big with wings that gleamed.

"Oh."

"With Mary."

Norma put her hand on the wire. The sleeve of her green suit pulled up. There were small streets cut into her arms. Where did those streets lead? "Mary again," she said.

"And my grandmother."

"I used to live out there. I did a lot of things. I drove a car and I cooked." I looked closer at Norma's wrists and I saw that the streets led into towns with buildings and a school and roads that led to houses with paths that led to doors. Every house had windows to see through and the gardens in the front had hoses and red buckets and cats and small children singing. All the weeds had been dug out and there were flowers along all the paths, every one with a bright skirt for dancing.

I wanted to make a visit. "My brother lives out there. He comes the first Monday of every month to see me."

"Oh," I said. Cain slew Abel and that is brothers.

"He doesn't understand why I want to stay here." I drew the shape of a brother with my finger across the wire. He had a stick like Abel's. In my drawing the brother held the stick high and said, "Be careful."

"I can't explain it to him. He thinks it should be him in here. He says, 'You're not living, Norma.'"

"You're not living, Norma," I said.

"Harrison is coming soon."

"Who is Harrison?"

"My brother. He's coming on Monday."

"When is that?"

"On Monday, silly." Mary flickered through Norma's eyes.

"Keep walking?" Norma asked.

"Keep walking," I said. We walked around and around with the rope that wasn't there tying our feet together. When air time was over I could still feel the rope.

I lay on my bed, first with my eyes open, looking for cracks in the ceiling in the shapes of wings, then with my eyes closed. I drew the tree of Boot growing down my arms and along my fingers until it broke through me, knocking me down. I drew handle and spoon. They spoke to me again for the first time since Sack turned my paintings into birds and they tried to fly away. My friends tickled my ears. It was all whispering; I couldn't hear the words. I drew the thin stick of Sack's body bending in, walking more on one side than the other. I drew the gray shadow pathways that ran under the skin of her hands. I drew the pink spider under Sack's eye changing from spider to fly.

Norma sat on one side of the morning room, I sat on the other; the cloud of smoke hanging between us. Norma lifted her hand, put the white stick to her mouth, and sucked. Through the cloud of smoke, her little fire glowed hot. I lifted my hand, put the white stick to my mouth, and sucked. My little fire glowed hot. Her hand went down into her lap. My hand went down into my lap. We watched each other; our eyes never looked away.

Every day we did the smoke dance and the rope that wasn't there around our walking feet tied itself around our insides and bound us to each other. Pictures ran in between. It was Mary and Norma, both.

At breakfast I never drank my pink tea. I did a switch with Rita who couldn't see, or I tipped it in my slipper when the blue shoes was at the trolley. All day my slipper was sticky but I never drank the tea; Norma said not to.

Nurse Clegg said, "Pool visit." It was under, where the hanging room should have been. The ladies walked in a line down the steps all slippery on the sides. Black birds sat along the railings leading down. If you made a sound it came back to you. Rita shouted, *Mup mup mup*. It came back, *Mup mup mup*. Blue shoes gave us white short pants and a top for the hills. Water was in a box. The ladies climbed into the water like John the Baptist going under.

"We live in a sea home. We sleep in sea beds. We have a sea baby," Norma said, flipping like a fish when the Red Sea parted. "Swim, Hester!" The sound bounced around the walls, *Swim Hester swim Hester swim Hester.*

It was Monday and Norma's brother was coming to visit. A visit is when you go for a while and somebody is there and you see them and then you come back. It's what I did with my grandmother. Visits end and you walk home and draw pictures of the things you saw. Sometimes the ladies here get visits. They go to the visiting room to get them. "Is Cain coming?" I asked.

"No," said Norma. "Harrison might bring Harvey, but if he does, Harvey will stay in the car. Sometimes he nips."

"Who is Harvey?"

"Harry's dog." Norma told me how she lived close to the bush when she was small. She said Harrison and her made a flying fox that took them across a river. She said you hung on and the tire flew along the wire. She said that the trees were filled with parrots like bright candies hidden in the branches. Every time you saw one you got a sweet surprise. They called to you and the chatter was a chorus of bells. Harrison and Norma made a secret place in an old wombat hole and they hid there when their father came and then one day Harrison got stuck by his foot and Norma rescued him with a car chain and all he had was a sore foot and he said it was worth it because he saw wombat bones and treasure. When she asked to see the treasure Harrison said it was guarded by a pirate with a hook for a hand. Norma's face broke into tiny drawings when she told this story. If she had laughed for longer I would have had time to look closely at every drawing to see what the pictures were. Then she said, "I have to go to the visiting room. Will you be all right?"

"What is all right?" Three black birds dived down. I shut my mouth tight.

"Your questions drive me crazy." Norma laughed. She was the happy sun. "I will tell Harrison about you."

I sat in front of the television and waited. A man read a story about an army in the dust and a bear being born. When Norma came back the sun was behind clouds. She sat down in a chair beside me and closed her eyes. A picture of Norma waving good-bye to her brother came down the rope to me. Norma didn't talk for the rest of the day. She stared straight ahead and sometimes she lifted up a corner of her mouth, but not to smile—to stop something.

I woke up to the scream of Norma traveling along the rope and into my ear. In the black eye of Norma's scream I heard a hot need. I got up from my bed and shouted loud. I kept shouting until I heard blue shoes coming to my room. I stood behind the door and when the blue shoes opened it I knocked them hard so that they fell behind me and I ran down the rope to Norma. I ran through a long worm, dark on all sides. Norma's scream pulled me on. I opened three doors and ran through. Blue shoes were behind me. They were chasing me but I was faster because I had to get to Norma.

She was in a room with other beds. The devil was on her, his black-scaled head bent in her neck, his flaming tail whipping back and forth. He wanted to eat her.

Norma was trying hard to get away from him but the devil was strong. He was biting her and growling in her ear.

"No!" I said to the devil. "No!" He lifted his head and showed me his sharp teeth. I came close and stood between Norma and the devil. "No," I said again. "Get away from Norma." The devil put his head on the side. "Get away!" I said. The devil left, hungry and low on his legs.

I got on Norma's bed, I whispered, "Norma K., Norma K., Norma K. is for Kyte but you don't fly it, you only say it if you want to, *Norma Norma Norma*." She went quiet and soft as a pillow in my arm. Her breathing slowed. She looked in my eyes. Her face was shining wet. The devil was gone. Blue shoes were on us; they dug a needle into the bone of Norma K. and they took me back to my room where they dug one in me. The needle scratched the bone until it made a hole, and when the hole in the bone was big enough the blue shoes gave a push and in went the mud, thick and heavy.

• • •

Norma wasn't in the smoking room in the morning. I asked a blue shoes, "Where's Norma K.?"

"In love, are you?" said one.

"Norma K.'s getting the royal treatment," said another. Tina did a royal curtsey and ladies laughed. The royal treatment was when the king came downstairs and ordered the death of Christ. Norma wasn't in the game room without the games, or in front of the television, or in the Airing Court. Norma K. was nowhere. I waited and with my eyes closed I drew pictures and sent them along the rope to Norma. I sent the green leaves on the other side of the wire, I sent our two feet walking, and I sent water from the pool visit.

Boot, why won't you look into my eyes? In a night visit you looked into my eyes at my full face, you put your mouth over mine, and then, after I woke up with blood flowers on the sheets, you never saw my eyes again. You saw Cat, you saw the pots and pans, the sink, the toilet, the bed, the walls, the Bible, the hanging room, the bucket, the axe, the pile of chopped wood, but not my eyes. Boot, if I came back would you look?

A man inside the television said, "*Drink this and you can sit in a pool of water with me.*" A lady in the water said, "*Touch me,*" and an orange sang, "*I am the sweetest juice.*" I watched a spider on her web in a high corner of the smoking room. "Sweep away the web, Hester," Sack would say, holding out the broom. I stood on the upside-down bucket, reached up with the broom, and broke the home of the spider. No broom for me here, no Sack saying, "Sweep." A fly came and stopped on a strand of the spider's web for a rest from all that fast flying. When she went to leave her feet were stuck; it didn't matter how much she pulled. The spider came walking slowly across. He could see the fly trying to get free from the sticky strand of web. He smiled, put out his feet to the fly, and spun his web around it. For a while fly wriggled, and then she stopped. You couldn't see her after that because she was part of the spider.

Sack's eyes came to me in my room at night—two blue plates spinning with the pink spider waving underneath. What was it that spider wanted me to know?

After breakfast Pebblinghaus said, "You have a special visitor today, ladies, a student of psychology. Aren't you lucky?"

A lady with pink on her cheeks and eyes brown as tea without milk said, "Hello, I'm Alice Plow. You can call me Alice."

"Call me Alice," said Rita.

"Call me Alice," said Linda.

"Call me Alice! Call me Alice!" said everyone in the room. Alice Plow tried to smile. Rita jumped up and down and screamed, *Alice Alice Alice*. Blue shoes took Rita away and the room went quiet.

"How do you want to start this?" Pebblinghaus asked Alice Plow.

"I want to begin with painting."

"Painting? That will be interesting," said Pebblinghaus, with a small laugh. The laugh was a stick in Alice Plow's eye.

Alice Plow left it stuck there and tried again. "Yes, it's proving to be a useful technique. Deconstruction of the images can really tell us things."

"What things do you want to be told?" asked Pebblinghaus.

The pink in Alice Plow's cheeks turned to red. "It's a useful technique," she said. "Will you help me to distribute these?" Pebblinghaus closed her mouth and gave everybody a paintbrush. Alice Plow put colors on a tray—red, blue, and yellow. I looked at the shining colors with my back against the wall. Mrs. D. threw her paintbrush at Pebblinghaus. Annie put hers in her pants. Everybody else sat like me, back against the wall on a chair.

The wooden brush that I was holding tightly in my hand spoke to me. "Hold on," it said.

Alice put paper on the table.

Nan said, "*Bugger off.*"

Alice smiled and it hurt her face. "I want you to paint the way you feel today," smiled Alice Plow.

"Bugger off, Alice Plow!" shouted Linda.

"Bugger Alice! Bugger Alice!" Again the room was full of shouting. Pebblinghaus hid the devil's laugh behind her closed teeth. Linda stood, picked up the tray of colors, and threw them at the wall. Red, yellow, and blue splashed against the wall. A painting of a red lion trapped in a pit covered a corner. His tail dripped. There was shouting and running in the room. The blue shoes took Mrs. D. away too. I kept my brush in my hand and held on.

Alice Plow picked brushes up off the floor. She looked at the colors on the walls. What were they telling her? "Perhaps we'll start with something else," she said.

"Whatever you like, dear," said Pebblinghaus as she wiped up paint.

Alice Plow wanted to go back on the other side of the fence with the high thorns.

Norma came back. She was in the television room with a gray blanket around her shoulders. She wasn't looking at the box of tricks, or tapping her fingers, or pinching the person beside her, or smoking; she was looking at the wall. I sent her a picture of me waving but the picture got caught in a knot. Norma looked at the wall and I looked at Norma. I had a question for her. A black bird flew past the window. The blanket fell over one of Norma's shoulders. I walked to where she sat, one eye on the hungry bird. I stopped beside her chair. The bird's eye shone as he flew past. Norma was the sad moon. I pulled two white sticks from the elastic in my pants. I took a deep breath and asked my question: "Smoke, Norma?" The bird stopped flying and watched me. His beak could break the glass. I asked my question again: "Smoke, Norma?" She looked at me, very slow. Her face had a shadow and a cut and some of her hair was gone. I asked the question one more time, the bird outside tapping at the glass with his beak. "Smoke,

Norma?" I held out the white stick. She didn't take it. I put both white sticks into my mouth, struck the match against the box, and lit two fires. I put one white stick between Norma's lips. "Suck, Norma," I said. "Suck." Norma sucked. The fire glowed hot. She closed her eyes. God's peace was on its way. When she opened her eyes again she smiled at me through the smoke that curled from her nose and her mouth and I saw the dark gaps of her missing teeth behind the smoke. I smiled back. "Norma K.," I said. When I looked up at the window the bird outside had flown away. Norma sent a picture of herself waving *Hello, I'm back* down the rope to me, and this time there was no knot in the way.

It was air time and Norma and me walked the same steps, our feet tied together. The sun warmed our heads and the green leaves danced for us on the other side. Two white chariots passed on the road; I watched until they disappeared. Norma scratched at her wrists. "The devil always comes after I see Harrison. He had me in the bed but when you came to me he went away. He was gone before I got the shot." She stopped at the wire so I stopped too. "Nobody ever got him to go away before." We held onto the wire. "They zapped me anyway." Norma winked at me. Her green butterfly sat against the side of my hand.

I was in the pool with the ladies. None of them had faces; only Norma floating beside me had a face. A man wearing short pants and white socks stood on the side of the pool and put his arms over his head. Music played. Nurse Clegg said, "Do as Mr. Wills," and lifted her arms too. Some of the ladies without faces lifted their arms and some didn't. Norma splashed me, she was laughing. I splashed her back; white water filled the air. Some of the ladies turned slowly like Mr. Wills. Mr. Wills didn't have a face either; no nose or mouth or eyes. Air went into him through his skin. Norma jumped on my shoulders and we went under. I opened my eyes. Norma was laughing under the water. She was soft at the edges as she moved. We stayed under there for a long time. When we came up the ladies and Mr. Wills and Nurse Clegg were sleeping on the shore. The breath went slowly in and out through their skins because they had no faces. Norma and me were in our own land; it was a water land where you never had to lift your arms or make a smooth transition. We ran over round black stones and then we grew fish tails and dived into the water.

Nurse Clegg gave us cleaning duties. I got the job of washing around the sinks. Brown sticky sink dirt was caught under the taps and it was my job to take it away. I put the sponge in the bucket and then I wiped under the taps. The brown dirt came off the white tiles and went into my sponge. The small holes in the sponge were little round beds for the dirt. The dirt moved from one place to another place. It was my job to move it. My sponge had changed color now that it was a house for sink dirt. How would you ever get the dirt to go away for good? It never goes away; it just changes houses. "Get on with it, Hester." A blue shoes came close. I kept wiping.

We were walking around the Airing Court. Norma talked while I kept watch for black birds. "I can do a lot of things in the outside world; I mean, I used to." Gray clouds filled the sky. "I could drive a car and work in a shop. I worked on a boat once, with my brother. I cooked. I had my own money— but I could never tell when the devil was coming. It's better to be here than out there. He could really get me out there, and I never knew when." Soft rain began to fall. "I tried to kill myself. More than once, I tried. That's why I'm here. I don't have to be here. I can leave anytime. I could be living with my brother. He lives near a river and he fishes. He used to live in the city, but he had a breakdown, because of what happened when we were kids. It happened more to me than to him. When I see him it reminds me. But I can't stop seeing him. He's my baby brother. I've got money from when the house was sold. My brother has it saved. I told him to spend it. I told him I'm never leaving here. I'll go to hell if I leave here." Norma's face was red. "You saved me the other night. You are my saving angel." Her eyes were a mirror and in the mirror I could see myself. I was made of light and I flew through the rain like Gabriel with a message.

∙ ∙ ∙

I woke up; handle, axe, spoon, broom, stairs, tree, and table all called to me at once. Their voices filled the room. I wanted to answer them, but because they all spoke at the same time it was hard to know who to talk to, or what they were saying. The room was full of whispers, then shouting, then back to whispers. "Handle," I said, because he was my first friend. "What are you saying?" Handle went to answer but spoon jumped in, and then broom; they laughed and whispered so that I couldn't hear handle. "Quiet!" I told them. "Handle, what are you saying?" When he went to answer the wood going into the red wood stove called out to me so loud that I had to cover my ears with my hands. I went to sleep; when I woke no light came through the square cut out of my door. I couldn't hear the talk of blue shoes in the hall, I couldn't hear the television in the nurse's quarters, or the shouting of ladies lost and looking for a hanging room. It was a black and empty space between other spaces. Something just for me was coming. It was one voice made of all the voices I'd ever heard. "Go home."

I kept the brush from Alice Plow's visit hidden in my pants. On the end of my bed I painted Norma and me on the spoon-boat. We were all yellow and made of stolen breakfast yolk and we sailed through the neck of the bottle together.

"What do you want, Hester? I want to give you something."
Norma sat beside me while dogs jumped through hoops in
the box of tricks.

"What is something?" I asked.

"Something I can do for you," she answered. The dogs
jumped through the highest hoop. The hoop was on fire.

"What?"

"That's what I am asking you. The devil hasn't been back
since you came here and stopped him. What can I do for you?"
I didn't know what she wanted me to say so I didn't say anything. "Hester, what?" I wished there to be an answer. I didn't
know what she wanted. There was no answer in me. "There
must be something I can do for you. You saved me, what can
I do for you?"

I started to cry. I didn't know what Norma wanted. The
crying was loud. I don't know why it was there. I waited for
Norma to hit me with her hand. Norma leaned over and put
her arms around my neck. She put her head on mine. Our
two hard heads pressed together; it was warm in between. I
heard the sound of hair rubbing hair. My crying kept coming. "I'm sorry, Hester," she said. "I didn't mean to scare
you."

When my crying stopped and we looked up, two men in
the television were patting the dogs that had jumped through
the hoop of fire. One of the dogs had a burnt tail. They gave
that one a gold coin on a ribbon and a biscuit.

. . .

Norma told me about going on a boat. She said she did the cooking and every night she looked in a book for what to make and every night it was different. Sometimes it was pie with onion and bacon, sometimes it was roast pork with crackling, sometimes it was apple pie with cream. She said she could see the ocean through the window as the boat sailed along and she used to stir in time to the rocking of the boat. Everything was salty and she saw a whale, which is the biggest of the fish, too big to belong to any person. It belonged instead to the ocean. I asked, "How many animals fit on the boat?"

"Just my brother and a crew of six. That was enough."

I lay in my bed the boat. We sailed over the seas to my grandmother in the water cemetery. Headstones floated on the surface of the sea. When my grandmother saw Norma and me she said, "At last." She climbed on my bed and we sailed away while Norma stirred the custard in time to the waves that rocked us.

When I woke in the night, tree was standing by my bed. Her branches touched the ceiling and her dry leaves crackled softly in the small breeze that blew. "Hester—pretty, beautiful Hester," she whispered.

I got out of bed and put my arms around her. She was cool and rough; the lines in her body told me stories through my skin. If tree kept growing she would knock down the walls and push off the roof as she reached for the land of the sun. If tree kept growing Renton would fall. "Hello, tree."

"Hester," tree said. Her voice had a lonely tear falling because back at One Cott Road she only had Boot's empty wet shirts to talk to.

"Hello," I said.

"Hester, come home to us," she said.

"But I am here, in Renton."

"Ask Norma. Come home—just for one night."

"But we are in Renton."

I lay back down and closed my eyes. Tree's leaves crackled as they sang a sleep song just for me. "Ask Norma," she said one more time before it was morning and she was gone.

I sat beside Norma at the breakfast table and listened to the sound of bacon being chewed. One lady was asleep with bacon in her hand. Norma took the bacon from the lady's fingers, put it in her mouth, and winked at me as she chewed.

I put down my bread and said, "Norma, can you take me home?" A black bird hopped onto the table and pecked at Rita's crumbs. She didn't stop him; she was talking to a friend you couldn't see. "What a man you are, what a great, great man you are!"

Norma turned to me. "What?" she asked. I could see the bacon turning somersaults in her mouth.

"I want to go home."

"I can't take you home."

Nurse Clegg poured the pink water into our cups. "Take me home, Norma," I said when Nurse Clegg was past my cup.

"What are you talking about?"

"I want to go home."

"They don't want you at home." Norma licked bacon oil from her fingers. "Home's over."

"Take me home."

"If they wanted you at home, you wouldn't be here."

"Home for one night," I said.

"Why?"

"One night."

Norma shook her head. "You don't make any sense."

"One night," I said again.

"I heard you," she said, so I stayed quiet. Norma had heard me.

I was in the game room without the games, making pictures with closed eyes, when Pebblinghaus came to me. Her metal hair shone like a fork after a polish. "Hester, you are to be moved into the dormitory. There is no need for you to be isolated at night any longer. Nurse Clegg will take you to your new bed tonight. I am sure the transition won't cause you any problems."

Spoon whispered, "Good."

Norma asked, "What was that all about?"

"Take me home—one night."

"Not that again." Norma walked to the other side and leaned on the wall with one foot up. I watched her, and waited.

I sent pictures to her down the rope; me and Norma in the sea, me and Norma in the forest, me and Norma going home for one night.

Nurse Clegg took me to my new bed. It was in a row of other beds with the long bump of a lady sleeping in every one. The bumps rose and fell like waves on a sea of sleep. "In you get," said Nurse Clegg. "Quietly now." I climbed into the bed and lay on my back with the blanket tight around my chest. The music of sleep was all around me. It was pipes, trumpets, and whistles. Sleep pulled me into the dark sea; a fish face swam close to mine and then Norma started to talk, pulling me back up to the surface. "Go away," she said, "please *go away!*" I could smell bacon left alone too long, and floor-water. It was the devil coming. "No, no, please go away!" said Norma. I pulled back my blanket and quiet as Cat mouse-hunting I crept to her bed before he got there. "It's Hester," I whispered.

"Hester, Hester." Norma held on to me. I turned to the devil; he had black hands like in *The Abridged Picture Bible* when Jesus faced the tower. His ears were hard sticks. He was hungry for Norma. "No," I told him. He showed me his teeth. "No." He shook his head; his eyes flashed white at me. "No," I said again. He scratched at the air in front of my face and made a low growl. "No," I said. He looked at me with his head on the side. "Go away," I whispered. The devil blinked two times, then turned and left the room.

"Only you can save me." Norma wouldn't let go.

"Please, take me home for one night," I said, then I crept, quiet as Cat mouse-hunting, back to bed.

When I woke again there were dry leaves across my pillow, one on my cheek. I rubbed my eyes. Tree was making a visit. My friends hung from her branches by ropes knotted around their necks. There were spoon and broom; there were axe, handle, and pencil. They turned very slowly in the breeze that blew. "Come back," they called. "Come home."

Norma and me looked out the window from our two chairs. Cloud moved, showing sun then hiding sun. Our two paths of smoke curled up from our mouths and twisted around each other. Norma's butterfly opened and closed its wings in time to the sun's coming and going. "I want to go home."

"No."

"Please take me home."

"They don't want you, they'll send you straight back."

"Please take me home."

"How can I take you home?"

"Take me home."

"Why?"

"One night."

"What do you mean, *one night?*"

"Home for one night."

"How can I take you home?"

"You can take me."

"How?"

"You can do it."

"What do you want to do in one night?"

"Go home."

"But *why?*"

"For one night."

"What do you want to do in one night, Hester? What do you think you're going to find?"

"My wish."

"What's that?"

"Home."

"But—"

"I will find it."

"Find *what?*"

"My wish."

"Will anyone know you've come home?"

"No."

"How will you get inside to find your wish?"

"The hidden key."

"Oh God, Hester."

"Quiet as a mouse."

"What will you be looking for?"

A black bird flew in a circle over Norma's head. He gave a hungry squawk. "Home." It was my last word.

It was night and Norma came to my bed. "Let me in," she whispered. I lifted the blanket and Norma climbed in. "I don't care if they catch me," she said. "You stop the devil in his tracks." She lay close and it got warmer in the bed as our breath mixed.

Norma rolled onto her back and told me what a waterfall is. She said you stand under it on a smooth gray rock and the water splashes down on your head and it never empties, it pours and pours. It pours over your hair and pulls it back off your face. It splashes onto your eyes and when you open them you see everything for the first time and it glows with the newness. The water pours over your front and arms and back and legs and all your old skin is washed away over rocks and a new skin comes from underneath. It is pink and clean because nobody has touched it or lied to it or used it. The old skin is washed down to a pool where it drops to the bottom and become pebbles that make a round floor to hold the water from the waterfall. She said she went to a waterfall when she was a girl. Harrison was there, she said. "All my best memories, my brother is there."

Her voice whispering in the dark made pictures of the waterfall shine above our heads. We didn't speak for a long time as the water fell down over us. Just as I was going to sleep I asked her, "What is a brother?"

"A brother is from the same blood."

"Am I your brother?" I asked her.

"No, silly." She put her arm across me. "You are my sister."

"Will you take me home?" I said. Norma didn't answer that question.

We slept and in the morning a blue shoes woke us and said, "Bloody hell, you two."

My friends called to me all the time and every voice was mixed with tears. Broom told me he couldn't sweep; the dust flew out from under him and wouldn't stay in a pile. Spoon said she had no strength to push the meat around. Axe told me that when he went to chop the wood fell off the block and wouldn't stay still. Handle was stiff and wouldn't turn, and back door wouldn't open. Table said her knees were weak. Tree cried. She said, "Come home, ask Norma, ask Norma."

"But Norma said no," I told her.

"Ask again," she said, then kept up her crying.

I went to Norma's bed, "Norma?" I whispered.

She woke up. "What is it?"

"Norma, will you help me?" Help is what Jesus gave to the hungry. He said, *Mary, I forgive you* and Mary and Jesus stood under a waterfall together. He set her free, he led the people out, he helped everyone nailed to the cross to climb down. He gave them an orange to eat in the desert. In *The Abridged Picture Bible* the desert was yellow with a camel and nothing else. The sun burned down and Jesus changed the desert into paradise with a green leaf.

"What?"

"Help me." Tree was using my mouth as her crying hole.

"Ssshhh. Hester, stop crying, what is the matter?"

"Help me." Tree kept crying through the hole.

"I want to help you. Please stop crying."

"Help me."

"I want to help you. Stop crying or a blue shoes will take you to isolation."

"Please, please, help me." Tree's long moan came out of my mouth.

"What can I do?"

"Take me home."

"Hester . . ."

"You can do it."

"But—"

"Do it. Help me."

"But—"

"Please."

"I don't know if I can."

"You can."

"All right, all right. I will try and get you home. Now be quiet." Tree stopped crying and went back to sleeping in the garden. Gray air that had been stuck down in the deepest part since I left One Cott Road came out of my nose and mouth.

I told my friends I was coming home. They said, "But are you? Are you? When are you? If you are, then *when when when*?"

"I don't know when."

Axe spun on his head. "*I don't know* is not good enough!"

"*I don't know* is nothing," said spoon, jumping from the shelf. Pumpkin hit the walls.

"We need to know exactly when. When you will come. When?"

"But I don't know."

"Ask Norma," said tree softly. My friends filled all the spaces. Food wouldn't go in. I couldn't close my eyes; they were stretched as wide as I could get them to make room for my friends.

"Norma, when?" I asked her in the Airing Court.

"This is stupid," she said.

"When?"

"This is dumb."

"But you said yes."

"I had to get you to shut up. I had to say yes, but it's stupid. How can you go home?"

I vomited onto her feet. I held my hands to my ears as handle shouted, "I was your first friend, before Mary, before Mog, before Norma with a K, and you aren't coming! Traitor!" Handle started to cry. I sat in the game room without the games. A lady in the corner was hitting her head against the wall. She wore a helmet. I saw but I couldn't hear the sound of her head hitting because my friends from One Cott Road were too loud. Nurse Clegg and blue shoes moved their mouths; they looked at me and waved their arms in the air. I couldn't hear them and I didn't know what they wanted. One blue shoes gave me a push in the back. The river of blood broke its banks, spraying out my fingers wrapped around the neck of a blue shoes. A needle went deep in my bone and I woke up in isolation. There was no face on the wall with hands to count as they turned. I lay in the bed and counted nothing at all. Was it one day that I lay there? Was it a single tick? Was it eighteen years? Blue shoes came into the room. They strapped me to the bed with brown belts and then one blue shoes rubbed oil onto both sides of my head and put a needle in my bone. Cloud came out of the sky through a small window and started to fill the room from the floor up. Another blue shoes put wires to both sides of my head, where the oil was. A man stood near a box. He said, "Set for operation." The world lit up and sent me stiff. Then it went black. Everything finished.

When I came out there were blankets of cloud around me. I could reach out through the cloud but nobody could reach in to touch me. A blue shoes sat me on a chair. Ladies moved around me. Norma came over; she took my hand but I couldn't feel it because of the cloud blanket—I could only see it.

"Hester, I am sorry. Can you forgive me?" I looked out through the window. The sun had roads coming out from his face like the hands came out from the face of the clock. I watched the roads turn as they came through the window and passed over my leg. "Hester, speak to me. I broke a promise to you and I am sorry. Say something." In Norma's eyes there was water. Behind the water, behind the eye, Mary waited.

"What happened to you? Where are you?" The light was moving up from my foot to my knee. It was a hand from the clock of the sun as it measured time passing from eternity. "Hester. It is terrible without you. I am sorry. I will get you home. I will do everything I can to get you home, if that is what you want." The sun hit me full in my face.

Spoon lifted her toes and danced around the bowl. "Yes! Yes! Yes!" Axe jumped and spun on his sharp shiny head, "Chop! Chop! Chop!" Broom laughed his way across the dusty floor. "Sweep! Sweep! Sweep!"

I turned to Norma. "Thank you."

"Harrison is coming again," she said. "I'm going to ask him to help." She took my hand; it felt warm and joined me to the living Norma. "Which blue shoes am I going to have to fuck for this?" She smiled at me, and winked. Her tooth gaps showed.

It was a Monday and Harrison was making his visit soon. Norma and me walked in time around the Airing Court. "I'm going to ask Harrison to leave a car waiting for us. Sunday nights it's only blue shoes—Nurse Clegg is off duty, that's when we'll do it, next Sunday. Mill Park, right? I'm going to try to get us out the back, through the kitchen, down to where the garbage goes." I watched another chariot disappear down the road outside the wire. "I don't want this to get us into trouble. I want to stay at Renton. This is the only place I'm safe—nowhere else—so nothing can go wrong."

"No."

"If it fucks up, if they make me leave, I'll kill myself. And if they make you leave I'll kill myself too."

"Nothing will go wrong."

Norma held my hand tight. "I'm glad I'm helping you," she said.

"Yes."

She let go of my hand. "I have to fuck a blue shoes to get the key for the kitchen. I'm going to steal it from him." Norma scratched at the small streets cut into her arms, knocking down five houses and a school. She looked across the Airing Court where a tall blue shoes with a snake on his arm stopped a fight between Mrs. D. and Annie. Norma knew a tree lived in his trousers with keys dangling from its branches. "I don't know why you want this so much. Those blue shoes stink." She snorted and I heard Mary laughing.

Suddenly my friends spoke so loud that I couldn't hear Norma when she talked. I saw her mouth moving but all I could hear was table, axe, Cat, tree, spoon, and handle calling me, "Hester! Hester!"

"I'm coming," I tried to tell them. "I'm coming." But I could only whisper because I didn't want the blue shoes to put a needle in the bone and I didn't want Pebblinghaus to put me back in isolation where I couldn't hear Norma breathing at night.

"It's all right, Hester. It's all right. We're going. I'm taking you. Just forget it for now. Look." She opened her hand and showed me a red beetle with black spots. "She came from the outside. This ladybug came a long way just to meet us." Norma turned her hand, and we watched the ladybug walking around Norma's hand, up her arm, and across the streets of the towns on her wrists. Then the ladybug spread her wings and flew out of the towns and through the wire in the fence. Norma lifted her arms. "Fly," she said, "fly." I lifted my arms and flew after Norma, three times around the wire.

When Harrison was visiting Norma I made a painting without paint on the toilet floor of Norma, Harrison, and me. We were under the water. We had a house there in eternity. Harvey was with us; he had wings and a fin and he nipped the devil when the devil tried to visit.

•　•　•

After I counted the hands around the clock eight times Norma came back from the visiting room. Her face was white with a gray shadow. A blue shoes told us to go to dinner. "Stay close to me," said Norma when we stood up to go. "I can feel him coming."

I stayed close. I could smell him too—sour milk and cat bone. I sent a picture down the rope of a circle around Norma. In the circle were Harrison, Harvey, and me. A vine of green leaves and purple grapes was wrapped around us. When the black-scaled hand of the devil came around a corner I said, "Go away."

Norma kept her hand on my knee through dinner. It shook. She only ate one piece of bread and she drank her pink tea and she drank my pink tea too. She didn't talk. She was asleep in her bed before the lights went off. From my bed I listened to the air being dragged in and hissing slowly out. I stayed awake to see if the devil came for Norma. Sometimes I smelled him and that's when I watched the closest.

It was morning in the smoking room. "The devil never came last night." Norma blew out smoke.

"No," I said. "He didn't."

"I can't live without you." Norma smiled and sucked. "My brother is leaving a car for us five nights from now. He didn't ask questions. Just like me; I'm not asking too many questions either. I have to get a key first, from a blue shoes. If I don't get a key then we can't go."

"Take me home."

"I am taking you home."

"Home."

"You won't have long in there. Do you realize that? Is there going to be enough time?"

"What for?"

Norma looked at me. "I don't know. To find what you want."

I painted a picture for Norma with Alice Plow's brush and toothpaste with water for paint on the end of Norma's bed when blue shoes couldn't see. I painted Cat, Norma, and me living in a house of pencils and brushes. The ladybug was our chariot and she took us back to One Cott Road.

Norma, me, and the ladies were in the pool. The tall blue shoes with the snake on his arm was standing on the edge watching over the wet ladies. Norma got out of the pool and went to him. She stood close to him, water dripping down her legs and face. She touched him on his chest and laughed as if she shared a secret with the blue shoes. He laughed too, as if the secret felt good to know. When Norma got back in the water she winked at me. "How long can you hold your breath?" she asked, before going under.

Alice Plow was at Renton again. Pebblinghaus came into the game room without the games. The glass on her fingers sparkled. "What do you want to do with them today, Alice?"

"I want to try painting again." Alice didn't look at Pebblinghaus. She looked at the ladies sitting at the big tables.

"Painting? That had some interesting results last time."

"Not quite the results we were hoping for, but today we might have more luck."

"Luck's not a word synonymous with Renton, Alice, but you're the boss."

Alice Plow looked into all the ladies' eyes around the edges of the tables and into my eyes too. "I'm going to ask you this time—who would like to do some painting today?" She had brushes in her hand. Even the people who were always talking to friends nobody could see went quiet. "Anybody? You might enjoy yourselves." The room was very, very quiet. Nobody wanted a needle in the bone. "Anybody—does anybody here want to paint? I'm not going to force anyone into this, but I do think some of you might enjoy yourselves." There was only the sound of the television telling us to eat cheese and insure the household. "Anybody?" She held out brushes. Pebblinghaus watched. My body with its arms and legs and feet and neck and head leaned toward the brushes in her hand. Alice Plow looked happy. "Do you want to paint?" she asked me. Pebblinghaus shook her head but Alice Plow put the brush in my hand. "Now you need some paint." She held up three bottles—red, yellow, white. Blood, the sun, and an egg. Alice Plow shook the bottles. "Which one?" I pointed to the egg. Alice Plow poured shiny wet white on a tray, then she spread brown paper. "Dip the brush in the paint," said Alice Plow. She didn't need to; I was already dipping.

I painted one white egg, then painted me and Norma inside the egg. It took up all of the paper. Alice Plow looked at my egg and she smiled. Then she looked at Pebblinghaus, pointed to the egg, and said, "Beginnings."

Every night I lay in my bed and counted another finger. Every day Norma said to me, "The devil doesn't come because of you. I owe you something and this is going to be it." My friends from One Cott Road called and called. The black birds flew over Renton all day and all night, waiting for me to speak. The only time I tried to speak was with Norma.

When I got to the thumb she came to my bed after lights out. "I will be back in an hour with the key. Tonight is the night. The car is waiting for us." I could hear Jesus beat the drum inside her *beat beat beat* and then he beat the drum inside me too so I couldn't tell what was Norma and what was me. "Wish me luck," she said, and then she was gone. I lay in bed with my eyes wide open. Tree, spoon, and handle were quiet; they knew that I was coming. I sent a picture of Norma and me and the egg down the rope to Norma in the nurses' quarters where she was stealing a key that hung from a branch in the trousers of a blue shoes.

I counted the beats of my drum and when I ran out of numbers Norma came back; she smelled of hot skin and toilet.

"Hurry, Hester. Get up and come with me." She took my hand and led me down between the rows of beds.

Annie woke up. "Where are you going?" she called, sitting up in her bed.

"Shut up, go to sleep." Norma pulled me along past the sleeping ladies. She undid the door at the end of the rows of beds with the key and we walked fast down the hall. It was bright light but we didn't see any blue shoes and Nurse Clegg was home with her feet up. We turned a corner at the end of the hall and went through another door. I heard sounds of metal and wood and the voices of ladies in the hanging room that I could never find. It was somewhere over our heads. "Don't slow down, Hester." Norma pulled on my hand and our fast walk became a run. Handle was calling to me, and just behind his voice was the voice of back door. "Come on, Hester, come on." I heard them as I ran through the halls and across the shining floors of Renton with my hand tight in the hand of my friend, Norma. We ran past windows cut into doors and the windows cut into doors ran past us, but they ran backward into the *before*, while me and Norma ran into the *next*.

We turned into a hall that took us to the kitchen doors. Norma undid the doors with another key. "Through here, quick!" Inside, the kitchen was dark and smelled of old butter and chops. We had to feel the way to go with our hands. Norma knocked against a bench and then I did too. Hard metal trays hit the floor with a crash. Norma and me stood in the middle as the crash bounced off the walls around us, growing louder. If the river of blood that flowed inside me burst, there would be nothing to hold it, no ocean for it to flow into. It would pour out over the world and all the people and animals would drown in it the way they did when God brought the mighty storm. Noah was the only one to get away. He packed a giraffe, his wife, and a horse and only *he* made it. He made it—he was free to start the new world, to grow the new wheat and chaff and breed sons and see the sun again and all of it began with him who got away. Before there was Noah, the water was deep and dark in a time of trouble. I swallowed, and wrapped my arms around my body tight. The kitchen went quiet again; I could only hear Norma breathing hard.

"Careful!" she whispered. "We have to be careful. Come on." She got to the doors at the back of the kitchen. "I hope this does it." She tried the key. I heard it shaking in her hands then I heard it hit the floor. "Oh God, oh shit." Norma went on her hands and knees and felt for the keys. "I can't find them." She crawled across the floor. "I can't find them, Hester. Oh God, where are they?"

I got down too. I felt with my hands under the shelf and I touched the cold scared keys. I passed them to her. "Here, Norma."

"Thank God," she said, and took them from me. She tried to put the key in the door again but the door said *no*. "Wrong key, I think it's this one . . ." She tried another one and the door opened *yes*. "Down these steps and then one more door." We went down some steps and I heard the hanging room table. "Not much further now," she said. There was no time to stop and talk to table. If me and Norma stopped we would turn as hard and salty as Lot's wife stuck on the cliff, not going or coming, only looking back for more of us that we would never see.

Norma opened the last door and the smell of garbage from the bins hit me in the nose as we stepped into the forbidden outside. I looked up into eternity to where Sack sent my paintings—lost paper birds flapped around the stars looking for me. I watched them circling. The hook of the moon hung in the black. I wanted to sail through the neck of the bottle to God the Bird where he waited, soft wing outstretched, eyes shining.

"Come on, Hester, we have to hurry." Norma pulled me down a small street between walls. "He said he'd leave the car down the side lane . . . just down here . . ." Buildings leaned in over Norma and me and, at the top, between them, eternity beckoned. A white chariot waited for us on the narrow road. Norma ran her hand over the roof of the chariot. "Get in," she said, as she opened the door where the wheel was. I opened the door behind her. "What are you doing, Hester? Get in on the other side, next to me." I did what Norma said and climbed in beside her. "The key should be under the mat . . ." Norma reached down to where her feet were. "Got it." She put the key in under the wheel and the chariot rumbled the way Boot's did. "So far, so good." Norma turned to me. "Are you ready for this?"

"I am ready for this," I said. Steam curled around my words. A black bird thumped against Norma's window when I spoke. Norma turned the wheel and the chariot turned into the road.

• • •

Two lights at the front of the chariot lit up tiny knives of water falling from the black sky. On both sides of the road trees stood like tall guards waving with their silver leaves. The road in front disappeared underneath us. I looked behind, into the darkness, but the road was gone, eaten by the chariot. Black birds cut through the chariot lights. Cold came off the window to sit on my nose, knees, and hair, but inside me, where Jesus beat the drum, I was hot.

"You never told me what you are going back to find, Hester. Are you going to tell me?" I didn't say anything because I didn't know what she wanted me to say. "What are you going back to find?" Norma's question floated around the warm dark space of the chariot looking for an answer but the answer was a secret that nobody knew, kept hidden down in the deepest part. The question was sucked out through the crack at the top of the car window and disappeared beneath us along with the road.

We drove for a long time without speaking. The only sound was the low growl of the chariot. Then Norma's voice came out with tears mixed through, the way milk runs through dough when you make the bread. She kept her hands on the wheel and her eyes on the road as she spoke. "I never loved anyone but my brother. He had short legs and apple hands. He sat on my back when we walked through the paddock on our way home from the shop and fed me candy. He'd reach around with a purple jelly baby in his fingers because he knew they were my favorite and say, *One for Norma.* I dressed him and he slept beside me at night and made the bed warm even in winter. I only loved him; there was nothing and nobody else that I loved ever. I never loved my mother and I never loved a dog. I never loved anything I owned, there wasn't a dress I loved, or a doll, a special thing . . . A grandmother. I met my grandmother. She scared me. Her teeth were brown and she said, *Why you?* I never loved my father; when he was at home his door was closed. My mother brought him in food on a tray. When she went into the room she was smiling; when she came out she cried. There was never any money for anything. One day my father brought a man to the house. He said to the man, 'Pay first.' The man wanted my brother but I said, 'Take me, take me,' because my brother was the only one I loved. The man turned me inside out so that my blood, heart, and brains were on the other side of my skin. I had nothing holding me together. Everywhere I went I dripped. I left a trail. That's how the devil knows where to find me; he follows the trail.

"The man came whenever he wanted and so did his friends. After that everything frightened me. I did things, I worked and lived in a proper house, but I was always scared. I wanted to die." She looked across the dark chariot at me. "Even smoking I don't love—I just like." We drove for a while more in silence, then Norma said, "I never knew if I was meant to be here. Who put us here?" Norma's question curled around our faces like smoke. It floated up in changing circles, it spread, it became thin, too thin to see. The question drifted into all parts of the chariot, thin enough to pass out the windows and into the sky. Norma and me were quiet—held inside the question as it spread out over schools and hospitals, houses, gardens, ladies, and fathers and blue shoes and grandmothers lying in cemeteries. Soon she sniffed. "I'm not scared now. I could go anywhere with you."

We went back to quiet and then Norma started to sing a soft song. "*Dance then, wherever you may be/I am the Lord of the Dance said he/and I'll lead you all wherever you may be/and I'll lead you all in the dance said he.*" I listened and then I made a small hum. Norma sang louder. "*Dance, then, wherever you may be* . . . Sing, Hester!" Her tooth gaps showed through the dark. "*I am the Lord of the Dance said he.*" I remembered my teacher with her smile that made a bridge for walking. I remembered the sting of Boot's night visit and I remembered the Lord of the Dance. I tried to sing but my voice was stuck behind a door. "Sing!" said Norma. "Sing!"

I pushed. "*Dance then . . .*" but the door was shut tight.

"Come on, Hester. I know you can sing. "*I danced on a Friday when the sky turned black* . . . Sing! Sing!"

I opened my mouth but still no sound.

"*It's hard to dance with the devil on your back!* Sing!"

My teacher stepped forward and pulled open the door. The sound flew out. "*They buried my body and they thought I'd gone/ But I am the dance and I still go on.*"

I sang loud and so did Norma. She opened up the window and the cold wind and the knives of water blew in and we sang our song loud together. "*They cut me down and I leapt up high/*

I am the life that'll never, never die/I'll live in you if you'll live in me/I am the Lord of the Dance said he."

When I saw lights out in the blackness we were quiet. "Smoke, Hester?" Norma passed me the box that was hidden in the top of her pants. I pulled two white sticks from the box, lit them both with Norma's lighter, then gave one to Norma. We sucked back the smoke. Norma kept the window open and the wind blew our hair, getting under our green suits, cooling our skin while the inside kept burning and the drums kept beating. Outside the chariot, eternity spread over our heads, all wide and black with tiny white holes that were the mouths of tunnels leading to the other side, to where God the Bird lived in the light. The smoke from our cigarettes rushed out the open window, curled up to the holes, and traveled down the tunnels. God the Bird cooked his worms over our smoke.

Norma picked a book up from the ground at my feet. "I need to look at this," she said. "We'll be there soon." She turned on a small light above her head and opened the book. She leaned forward and stared out the window at the roads leading off. "We're nearly there."

Soon I saw streets and houses that I knew from when I went to school and caught the bus. "This is your street, Hester— Cott Road." When we turned into the road my arms hurt from a hanging, my ear ached from where it was pulled, I stung down below, a tree grew through me, my knees were cracked from the floor, my hands burnt from the hot bucket water. I was home.

"Stop," I said to Norma.

"Where is your house?"

"Stop."

Norma stopped the car. "There's nobody around. That's good. There's so much empty land here. Why are there so many vacant lots?" Norma was asking questions but I didn't know what answers she wanted. "So where is your house?"

I pointed to the end of the road.

"All right."

I put my hand on the chariot door, to open it. Norma reached across and touched my shoulder.

"You know you haven't got long. Do you know you haven't got long? We have to get back."

"I know."

"How will you know when to come back?"

"I will know."

"But how?"

"By counting."

"Counting what?"

"I will know."

"But *how*?"

"I will know by counting the time. Boot taught me on the clock."

Norma looked at me like she was deciding something. "All right then. I'll be waiting for you."

I opened the door.

"You are coming back, Hester?"

"I'm coming back."

"Please come back. If you don't come back I don't know what I'll do. Promise me you'll come back. Promise me."

"I'm coming back." When I was at school I said to Mary, *I don't know you*, the same as Jesus's friend with his black hood in *The Abridged Picture Bible*, but it was a lie. "I am coming back, Norma K."

"Promise?"

"I promise."

"I need you." What is need? Norma was crying. Need was Hester coming back to Norma. She reached into the back seat and pulled out a dark blanket. "Take this, wrap it around you. It's cold out there." I wrapped the blanket around me as I stepped onto Cott Road. "Hurry back," she said through the open window.

Above me the moon hid behind sleeves of dark cloud. Rain fell softly on my head. I looked up and the rain fell on my eyes. I put out my tongue and tasted.

The hands of the clock had turned many circles since I walked down Cott Road; closer and closer to number one where I had grown big and dripped blood flowers and threw Boot at the wall. I pulled the blanket close around me and it turned me from Hester to shadow. I was a walking secret that had no sound.

There was only one streetlamp and everywhere was quiet but for my friends calling from One Cott Road. "I'm coming," I told them. "I'm coming." The dark branches of trees pointed the way home, with so many twisted stick fingers. "I know the way," I told them, my voice muffled under the blanket. I walked down a hill. At the bottom of the hill, apart from the other houses, with bush and grass on both sides, One Cott Road waited.

"Here I am! I came back to you, my friends!" I wanted to shout and run to the house but I stayed quiet because I was a secret that had to be kept. *Step step step* closer and closer.

"Hester, is that you? Is it you? Could it really be you?" cried One Cott Road.

Gray tears from her blinking window eyes dripped down the walls. Her front door mouth was down at the sides. "Where have you been?" she moaned.

"Renton," I answered. I was stinging and aching and itching in every part as I passed my hand along the wooden fence outside the house and angry fence splintered my skin.

One Cott Road snapped with her teeth of fence. "Why did you leave us?" I didn't know what the answer was. What is *why*? Is *why* when Boot and Sack take you to Renton? Is *why* the thing you were looking for? Is it the reason you came back? "Why did you leave us? Why did you have to go?"

"I am back now, I am home, shhhhh." I got to the high gate at the end of the fence and I opened her up wide. The high gate squeaked surprise when I walked through. I took the blanket from my shoulders and hung it over the fence; I was in the garden and there was tree. I ran to her and put my cheek to her trunk and the pictures that were drawn there— a feather and a leaf and a nest touched my face. "Pretty . . . beautiful . . . Hester," said tree. I cried and shook against the body of tree. I wanted to climb up her branches until I was at the very top and then I wanted to sail away to where she reached, to eternity and God the Bird. "Pretty . . . beautiful . . . Hester," tree said again. "Go inside."

"I want to stay with you." I pushed those words out past the tears that tried to stand in the way.

"Go inside."

"I don't want to."

"But you have to."

"But I don't want to."

"Hester—" Tree stroked my cheek. "You can do it, your friends are in there."

"But I don't want to."

"Go inside, Hester."

"But I . . ."

"*Go inside.*"

"All right."

"Good girl." I held tree tight for one more tick of the clock, then let her go and walked across the grass to back door.

"Hester," said back door, "you came back!"

"Yes," I whispered. "I told you I was coming."

"You kept your promise."

"Yes."

"The key is on the ledge. Stand on your toes and you can reach her."

"Thank you."

"Hester?"

"Yes?"

"I am happy you came back."

"Thank you." I stood on my toes and felt with my fingers along the ledge. I touched something hard. It was the key. She shook in my fingers because she was frightened. She sang a scared key song in my fingers—*Scared to go in scared to go in scared to go in must go in must go in must go in*. At night she always slept and never had a job to do until now that I was home. I pushed her, shaking, into the hole, and I turned her. Back door clicked and opened. "Welcome home," he said.

I stood in the kitchen of One Cott Road breathing the air. I breathed in dust, Sack, smoke, floor-water, the years before, the years after, soup on the stove, the hands of the clock, time ticking, stew in the pot, and the breath of Boot. Cat came and wound her black self around my legs. I picked her up and rubbed my face against her black-gray back. "Cat." I held her close and I put my ear to where her purr was. *You came back, Hester, purrrrrrrr.*

"Yes, I came back." I looked into her green cat eyes. I saw every mouse, bowl of milk, and bird dream that we shared. I saw our years under the table. I saw us running from Sack, our longing for the forbidden outside from the arm of the couch and our nights back to back under the blankets. All my secrets were in Cat's eyes. I kissed her black head. "Out you go." I put her through the open back door into the garden. She ran away into the darkness.

I turned on the small shelf light and I moved to the warm of the wood stove. I opened the heavy red door. I knew how; it was my duty. Inside the fire, only hot coals burned at the bottom. I had not been here to make the flames, but I was here now. I opened the wood box beside the fire. Chopped wood lay there in a lonely pile. "Hester! Hester!" They spoke together in happy voices. "You came back!" I took one wood out and held him to my cold ear. He whispered, "We needed you."

"Need is coming back," I told him. I pushed the wood into the burning coals and new flames danced. My face grew warm. I looked around the kitchen of One Cott Road; at the walls I washed, the floor I mopped, the stove I scrubbed, the ceiling I swept with the long broom to gather up the webs. I looked until I could close my eyes and still see what I had been looking at; so that the things I saw went deep inside to where they couldn't be found and taken away.

It was time to go to the hanging room and see the company I kept. I lit a prayer-for-the-dead candle with a match from beside the stove. The hanging room was a dark room; you needed light if you wanted to see the company you kept. I pulled open the door in the floor. She made a slow sleeping creak because nobody had opened her since Hester went to Renton. When I walked down the steps my arms hurt and I had to try hard to stop them flying upward. On my way down table called to me from the bottom, "You came back!" Jesus beat the drum from the feasts harder. My arms hurt more and more as I went down. When I got to the bottom I held up the candle and looked. They were all there; bars for hanging, rope for tying, table for standing on before I was hung, and the company I kept pasted to the walls. The drum beat hard enough inside me to break through me and play its own tune on the other side of my skin. Something else was inside me too—what was that thing that wanted to come out? What was it getting bigger and pushing up from the bottom? Was it eggs and porridge? Was it chops and peas? Was it the fish eye? It was a scream; it was coming, coming up through the tunnel that Jesus made his home in *The Abridged Picture Bible.* If it came it would scare the company I kept and it would wake the devil and he would come for Norma who was waiting in the chariot singing softly to herself, "Come back for me, Hester, and I will lead you in the dance." He would come for her and I would not be there to be the only one who could save her. I couldn't let that scream come out of my mouth. I pushed it down and it came out of my eyes instead, in hot salty water down my face as I looked around the hanging room at the company I kept. I was going to hang the way they were. I climbed onto the table and tied one of the ropes from the bar around my neck, the same as the ladies in the pictures on the walls. There was no Boot here now; I could kick away the table myself and hang. The rope was my necklace of thorns. I was about to do it when somebody spoke my name.

"Hester?"

Who was that?

"Hester?" The voice came again. Who was it? "Hester! You know me, Hester." It was a voice with a laugh hidden inside. It was axe. He was calling from outside the house where he leaned. "Come back upstairs," he said. "Come on." I could hang in the hanging room forever, still as Lot's wife. "Hester, get out of there!" If I hung I could have a small sleep. I could wait for the bird dream . . . "Come upstairs now!" Axe meant business. "Get out of there *now!*" I wiped my wet face, took off the rope, climbed down off the table, and walked back up the stairs.

When I got to the door in the floor she wouldn't open. She was stiff and sleeping again. I put down the prayer-for-the-dead candle and it blew out. It was black as Cat's back; I couldn't see my hands. I felt for the door and pushed but she wouldn't open. I pushed and I pushed; the scream was coming again. "No, no," I said to that scream. Again it sprang from my eyes. The dark curled around my cold sleepy shoulders like a blanket and made a warm bed for me. I rested against the wall. I wanted to stop and sleep like Cat on the back step.

"Hester, push the door open." Axe's voice came through the dark, brighter than a flame from a hot hungry fire, and woke me. "Come upstairs," he said.

"The door is stuck," I told him.

"Try again."

I tried again. Still the door didn't move. "It's stuck."

"Hester, if you push it hard it will open."

"It's stuck!"

"It will open if you push it hard, Hester."

"I did push hard. It won't open. I am going to sleep."

"No, you cannot go to sleep now. You can sleep later. Open the door."

"I tried. It's stuck. It won't open and I want to go to sleep."

"Stop your crying. Stop your crying right now and open that door."

"No."

"Open it!"

"No!"

"*Open it open it open it open it open it open it open it open it open it!*" Axe's voice split my ears and made cracks in my head. I pushed and pushed as hard as I could and the hanging room door opened. "Good," said axe. "Now come and get me."

I walked softly down the hall to back door. Handle smiled; the question was gone from his eye. He had no question anymore. He knew already. I turned him, opened back door, and went to the forbidden outside. The cold covered my face and crept in under my suit. Axe was leaning against the white wooden wall of One Cott Road, taking his night rest. "Good," he said, when he saw me. "You came."

"Yes."

"Take me in your hands." I took him in my hands and turned him. He was heavy and his shiny head sparkled. Axe was a boaster. I smiled at him and his tricks and his voice with the laugh hidden inside.

"Take me into the house," he said.

"What?"

"You heard me."

"You want to go inside?"

"That's right, I do. Take me."

"Why do you want to go inside?"

"Because I want to."

"Why do you want to?"

"It is my wish."

"But why?"

"I told you, because it is my wish."

"But what for?"

"Because."

"But why?"

"Hester, I am your good friend. I can give you pictures you've never seen before. Take me into the house. It is my wish."

"Something you want very much?"

"Yes, something I want very much. Let's go inside, Hester, you and me together."

I took him inside. We stood at the bottom of the stairs where I could see because of the shelf light in the kitchen. Up at the top of the stairs it was dark. I put my foot on the first step. It was the same shape as my foot from so much *up down up down* for the mop and the broom and warm tea with sugar bread for Sack with a bad back. I climbed onto the second step, then the third and the fourth. The smell of Boot and Sack's dreams got up my nose. Boot's dream was the smell of hair and trousers, Sack's was the smell of wet sponge. In Boot's dream he lived in a bottle; the bottle went down into the deep water, the glass of the bottle broke, and the water came in. Boot kicked his legs but he kept going under. Water filled his mouth and bubbled out his nose. It filled his body so that he grew so heavy that he sank to the bottom. In Sack's dream wings grew from her bad back. She flew to the forbidden outside where her wings hung her to the line by her nightdress with the faded flowers with only Boot's empty wet shirts for company.

When I got to the top of the stairs, all in darkness, I walked on mouse feet to my room. I opened the door and turned on the Christ light. The lamb and the lion were gone. The bed was there but no colored blanket. There was nothing of Hester left in the room. The scream pushed out my eyes.

"Hester." It was axe.

"What?"

"Stop crying. Let's go."

"Go where?"

"Into their room."

"Their room?"

"Yes. Don't pretend you don't know what I'm talking about."

"You want to go into their room?"

"Come on."

"Why?" I asked axe.

"Come on."

"But why?"

"What is *why*? Come on, let's go."

"But—"

"Let's go!"

"All right." At their door I heard them breathing. Sack's was a whistle, Boot's was a train caught in his throat. Axe and me made no sound. Axe was good at quiet, all that time leaning and sleeping and waiting for me to come home. I pushed open the door and I walked to their bed, creeping quiet as Cat when she sees the mouse with his head out the hole. As I walked I counted. It was Boot who taught me the lesson of counting, one for *this*, and he held up a finger, two for *this*, and he held up another, and three for *this*, and he held up the thumb. I counted on my own now. I got to seven and I saw them there by the light of the moon, Boot his mouth open so the tired air could drag in, and Sack on her side so I couldn't see her face.

"Lift me high," said axe, so I lifted. Jesus was in the corner on his chair. The lamb was at his feet, and the lion walked in a circle around him. Jesus smiled at me and I smiled back. He played the drum from the feasts and watched. "Higher," said that boasting axe. I lifted him higher over the sleeping Sack, who taught me the lessons of prayer and cleaning, and over the sleeping Boot, who taught me the lessons of trousers and tree. I had found what I was looking for. I had found the *why*. It was here in front of me. I could smell it, see it, and taste it. I was filled with the *why*. Time stopped ticking. The hands of the clock stopped turning. "Now," said axe. "Now now now now now now now now now now now now!"

I brought axe hard down into the head of Boot. I followed the cuts like he showed me. Boot rolled like a worm with a stick in his middle. He rolled and wriggled, one eye open. Axe took the other eye for his dinner. *There!* for your night visits, *there!* for your hanging, *there!* for your secret, *there!* for Mary without a friend but me, *there!* for your feet running whenever Sack called, *there there there!* I cut and I cut and I cut. Rivers broke their banks, Noah rose up in his boat, drowning men tried to climb on, but the blood rose in waves and the sides were too slippery. "Cut, cut, cut!" axe shouted. "More more more! Cut cut cut!" Jesus cried out to God the Father in heaven as Boot's blood covered the world. "Cut, cut, cut! More, more, more!"

Sack sat up holding her hands out in front of her. Boot's blood was in her eyes so she couldn't see properly. She tried to pull air into her body but it wouldn't go. She made the sound of a train pulling up at the station. Her eyes were open; the light behind the blood in them lit up the room in pink. Jesus stopped playing the drum and put his hands over his face. The lamb jumped onto his lap and hid in his robe. The lion stopped circling and watched.

I took axe to the side for Sack because her cuts went a different way. I swung axe hard through the neck of Sack. *There!* for your prayer, *there!* for burnt paintings, *there!* for fish eye, *there!* for the frog I never saw, *there!* for blood flowers on the sheets, *there!* for my grandmother at last, *there there there!* I cut and I cut and I cut.

"More more more!" Axe sparkled and shouted. His laugh was out; it bounced off the walls. "Cut, cut, cut! More, more, more! Cut, cut, cut!" The clouds parted in the sky, God the Father looked down at Sack in pieces, and watched as her blood joined with the blood of Boot and the world went under. The river of blood sprayed out through the holes that Boot's tree made in my head when it broke me open and my blood joined the blood of Boot and Sack. I made a red painting on the wall; I used my own hand. It was God the Bird with his crown of stones and me riding on his wing. We shouted, *Alleluia! Dance for joy!*

A new song sang itself in me. It had bells, a harp, and the angel Gabriel. Boot and Sack joined in. All the things you couldn't put a finger on that my skin held inside moved to the music of the new song. I stood sticky and wet, air going *in out in out* while Jesus played the drums and axe sang along.

I walked to the window and looked out at eternity made of moon, clouds, and stars. Dark smoky cloud crossed slowly, showing moon. Nothing ended; it went on and on. I climbed up onto the window ledge. If you jumped from the ledge you would fly up and into eternity, you would be a part of it, you would join with the lasting things, your eyes would be in the stars, your toes in the clouds, your hair would stream out over the world, you would never end, you would be eternal. I wanted to; it was a strong wish that pounded its way through my wet shaking self. I was about to jump out and sail through the neck of the bottle to where God the Bird lived when a picture came down the rope to me from Norma. It was Norma in the chariot waiting. Then there was another picture of

Norma and me and her brother. We sat by the river and though we couldn't see the frog we could hear him and his sound was a bubble that floated over the trees. I turned back to Boot and Sack.

I left axe beside Boot so they could talk and laugh because that axe was a funny, tricky boaster, then I took Sack's hair in my hand; I had never touched it before. It was a new thing in my hand. I closed my fingers around it; more blood than hair. I took her thin arm and I pulled Sack down the stairs; with each stair her body made a *thump* as if she was potatoes. I pulled her across the hall and into the kitchen, the same way Sack used to pull me down into the hanging room. I picked her up and held her close like she was Cat. Her body was as hard as a chair. I held her to me so tight that some of her might go through our two skins and into me. She didn't say not to. I put my ear to where her sticky mouth was, so I could hear her whispers. I waited for her to tell me not to, but she stayed quiet. I lifted her onto the table.

I went back for Boot. Boot and axe were talking. Axe said, "Hester is good at chopping."

Boot said, "Yes, she is."

Axe said, "She is a good girl."

Boot said, "Yes, she is."

Axe said, "She does a good job."

Boot said, "You are right, axe, she does do a good job. I showed her how."

Axe said, "You did, yes, you did. You showed her and now she is showing you."

Boot was heavier then Sack and he had no hair for pulling. I took him by his legs and I dragged him down. His back hit every step *bump bump bump*. He was heavy and wet with blood. I dragged him across the hall and into the kitchen to be with Sack because they were married everlasting. In the kitchen I didn't hold him close like Sack. Boot doesn't like blood and he had it all over him. I lifted him onto the table beside Sack. Their arms hung over, their feet hung over—it didn't matter what I did, the table was not big enough.

"Use me," said a voice from the cupboard.

"What?" I said.

"Use me, I have a hard edge for cutting." It was my old friend, knife. I took her from the cupboard and I turned her in my hand. Was that my wet, red face I could see in her blade? "Quickly," she told me. "Cut." I cut Boot and Sack. I cut through bone, I cut through skin, I cut through the things you couldn't put a finger on—secrets, laughter, pain—all leaked out and mixed with the puddles of blood on the floor. Now Boot and Sack both fit on the table.

I took the heavy pot and I put it on the red wood stove. I opened the door to the stove and put in more wood. Wood cried, "No!" as he burned.

"This is the last time. You have to." He understood. I put the pieces from the table into the heavy pot.

"My turn," said spoon from the ledge above the stove. She smiled at me with her round spoon face as I took her in my hand. We stirred the pot and sang together, "*The bread that I will give is my flesh/for my flesh is meat indeed.*"

"Enough," said spoon. "I need a rest." I lifted her out of the pot. I took a bowl from the cupboard, held it over the stove, and used spoon to fill it. The walls, the floor, the ceiling, my hands, the table were all red. I took a clean spoon for eating and I sat at the red table. I dipped the spoon into the bowl, lifted it to my lips, and I ate. The warm red milk ran down into the places that you couldn't put a finger on; down into the deep dark where it was all salt and tears from the eye of the fish, and it warmed those places *at last, at last.* I heard the songs of Boot and Sack; Boot like a trumpet heralding the beginning when Jesus rose again and Sack high like a pipe when the children danced in celebration on the next page.

Norma sent another picture down the rope. It was a picture of her smoking; the smoke filled the chariot so that Norma couldn't see outside. She didn't want to because the devil was in Cott Road, waiting to see if I would keep my promise.

"Hester!" Tree called me. I put down my spoon.

In the forbidden outside the moon showed tree standing alone, the knotted fingers of her branches reaching to eternity.

"Hester . . . pretty . . . beautiful." I went down to her and pressed my face to her so the drawings on her body scratched my cheek. "Don't cry, Hester," tree said to me. I put my arms around her and held on. "Don't cry, your time has come."

"I never want to leave you," I told her.

"I know," she said.

"Never."

"I know."

"Never, ever."

"I know, but you have to."

"What?"

"You have to go now. You have to leave me."

"Never."

"Hester, you have to."

"But that is not my wish."

"You have to."

"But I don't want to."

"Hester, you can help me get to eternity."

"How could I do that?" I asked.

"Set me on fire."

"No," I said.

"Yes, set me on fire."

"No, I don't want to."

"Set me on fire."

"No."

"Do it."

"No."

"Do it!"

"But I don't want to. You are my friend, you gave me pictures."

"Stop crying. I will give you one last picture. Let me go."

I looked up to where tree reached—up to the stars, the shining tunnels that led to the other side, where God the Bird waited. "Can I come with you?" I asked her.

"No," she said.

"Please."

"No, go back to the chariot."

"Why?"

"You made a promise."

"But I want to come with you to eternity. Please."

"No. Go back, you said you would. You made a promise. A promise is not a lie or a secret. You have to keep it."

I pulled away from the hard body of tree. "But I want to come with you."

"*No!*" Tree wanted to go alone.

"All right then."

"Good," said tree. "Stop crying."

"Good-bye," I said.

"Pretty . . . beautiful."

"Tree, I love you." I touched my face to the bark of her body one last time for one more story.

"Go," she whispered.

I went into the kitchen and found the water that Sack used to make a fire when it had rained all night and the wood was wet. I wet the house with the fire-water the way Jesus baptized

John and his friends. I wet the stairs and the floor. I ran upstairs and wet my room, I came back down, opened the door to the hanging room and splashed the stairs leading down as much as I could. I wet the company I kept. Fire-water dripped down their black-bagged faces. The eyes in the head of the lady looking up wept tears of fire-water. The ladies being stretched on the wheels were soaked—they floated in fire-water. The crowds of company watching the hangers were all drowning. I opened the door to Boot's study. Boats caught in bottles lined the shelves. I splashed them and they came crashing down from the shelves, cracking open. Matchstick boats flew up and out the window. They sailed up through the sky heading for the shining tunnels to take them to the other side. I went outside and put the fire-water around the body of tree. "Stop crying," she said as I splashed her.

Back in the kitchen I pulled fire out of the red wood stove with the hard pan. Some burned my hands. I put the fire on the bottom of the stairs, I put it all the places where I had splashed the fire-water. Spoon, axe, table, knife all called to me, "Good-bye, good-bye, your time has come." The kitchen was on fire. I pulled off my green suit, all red now. I left it on the floor and I walked out into the forbidden outside. The brush and laundry soap sat beside the hole for Boot when he came in dirty. I used the brush and the soap and I washed the red down into the plughole. Down it went in red-water circles, down to join the salty dark tears of the fish. I took the blanket from over the fence, wrapped it around my cold self, and went down to the high gate in the fence.

I turned back to look. Tree was on fire; her branches were hands of flame reaching up. God the Bird came through the black sky; his wings shone white against the darkness. One Cott Road was burning; yellow heat came from the windows. I wanted to stay there like Lot's wife. Still as hard salt, never needing to step forward or back.

Tree screamed as she burned, "Go away from here!" Her roots tore from the ground and she lifted up, bright with fire as God the Bird carried her away. It was tree's last picture.

I turned and ran. I took the path through the bush back to Norma. Thorns tried to pull my blanket from me, but I held on tight and kept running. I stayed in the dark away from the streetlamp.

When I saw the white chariot the devil was at the door. He was clawing at the windows and thumping the roof. The devil wanted to get Norma—he wanted to peel back her skin so her secrets dripped out, the way her father's good friends did. I could hear her screaming from inside the chariot, "No, please, no, please!"

When the devil saw me coming he jumped back, stopped in his tracks. We stared at each other, my breath coming from me *in out in out*. His breath steaming from his nose *in out in out*.

He came toward me, loping and fast. I was the only one between him and Norma. He wanted to pull me out of the earth's hold like a weed. But the devil had nothing for a weapon and I had my promise to Norma. I looked hard at every part of the devil as I ran toward him, eyes wide open. He was caught in my eyes. Nothing of him was hidden from me and I did not look away as I ran as hard as I could toward him. I held him prisoner in the light of my eyes, still bright with fire from One Cott Road. I watched him burn in their light.

The devil was gone, the air clear of his oil-and-bacon stink.

"Norma, it's me, let me in." I knocked on the door. "Norma, Norma with a K." The door opened. Norma was crying too much for words. "Norma, sshhhhh." I held Norma in my tight arms, her face damp in my neck.

"You came back," she cried.

"Yes," I said, "and now it is time to go."

"You came back."

"Yes, time to go, Norma."

"You came back without clothes, but you came back."

"Yes."

"Is he gone?"

"He is gone. Norma, let's go."

"Yes, okay." Norma started the chariot and we drove away from One Cott Road.

We drove in the dark without speaking as pictures ran along the rope between us. My picture to her was a house on fire. Her picture to me was the angel Gabriel. The black birds were gone. I fell asleep with my head against the window as Norma sang her driving song. "*I danced for the scribe and the Pharisee/ But they would not dance and they would not follow me/I danced*

*for the fishermen, for James and John / They came to me and the
dance went on."*

"We have to leave the car now. My brother will pick it
up before it's morning." Norma was shaking me awake.
"Quickly. We have to get you back to your bed. We have to
find clothes." Norma's voice shook as we got out of the car.
She held my hand and we went in through the back door of
Renton.

We went up the stairs into the dark kitchen. Norma was
pushing the keys into the lock when the light snapped on. The
blue shoes with the snake on his arm was waiting for us.
"Where have you been?"

"I did what you wanted," said Norma. The blue shoes had
fat on his neck. His collar was hurting it. "Let us get back to
the dormitory." Norma's hand was shaking in mine.

"You took my keys, didn't you?" The fat under the blue
shoes' collar spilled over.

"You can have them back." Norma threw the keys on the
floor near the blue shoes.

"Why hasn't she got clothes on?" He pointed at me as he
picked up his keys. "Where have you been?"

"Nowhere. Let us go back to bed." Norma held my hand
tighter.

The blue shoes stepped close and pulled the blanket from
my shoulders; it dropped to the floor. "What happened to her
clothes?"

"Leave us alone. I did what you wanted." Norma pulled me back from the blue shoes.

"You took my keys." Whenever the blue shoes moved his head the fat around his neck got squeezed harder. The snake on his arm made a lazy *hissssss*.

"You have the keys back now."

"What have you two been up to? Anything I should know about?"

"Nothing, let us get back to bed."

The blue shoes' eyes traveled across the hills on me, then he checked the clock on his wrist. "You better hurry." We went to step through the kitchen door but the blue shoes put himself in front of me. "Norma gave me what I wanted, but you didn't."

"Leave her alone. Let us get back to our beds." Norma sounded as scared as if the blue shoes was the devil.

"I'll let you go if you give me what I want." He was looking at me.

"There's no time," Norma said.

"Later there will be. I'll be coming for you later." He touched my shoulder; his fingers were cold. "And if you make trouble I'll have you both put in isolation."

"*I'll* tell," said Norma with her chin stuck out. "You're the one who'll be in trouble. You fucked me."

"Who do you think they're going to believe?"

Norma's face was red. "Bastard."

"I just want one more thing," said the blue shoes, touching my arm, "and then we can forget about it. Nothing ever happened."

"No," said Norma.

"I'd call it a fair deal—if she can be a good girl." The blue shoes touched my chin with his fingers.

"Leave her alone," said Norma. A spit ball jumped out behind her words.

I stepped closer to the blue shoes. "I can be a good girl."

Norma looked at me like I'd given her a surprise. "Hester, you don't have to."

"He will let us go."

"She's got the right idea." The blue shoes smiled.

"Yes," I said.

"I'll come for you," said the blue shoes. "I'll take you back to the dormitory now." On the way he took a new pants suit from the storage room. He watched while I stood in the hall and put on the new pants suit. He took the blanket. "Better destroy the evidence," he said, like we had a secret. "We'll go the long way so we don't get seen." Norma and me followed him the long way and never saw another person. When we got to the dormitory the blue shoes said, "I'll be coming for you." He opened the doors and Norma and me got into our beds.

"Good night, Hester," said Norma.

"Good night, Norma." I waited for the black bird to come and snatch my *good night* in his beak and fly with it out the window—but he never came.

Norma sat on one side of the smoking room, I sat on the other; the cloud of smoke hung between us. Norma lifted her hand, put the white stick to her mouth, and sucked. Through the cloud of smoke her little fire glowed hot. I lifted my hand, put the white stick to my mouth, and sucked. My little fire glowed hot. Her hand went down into her lap. My hand went down into my lap. We watched each other. Our eyes never looked away. There were no black birds anywhere. My friends didn't speak to me. There was a new silence in their place. Behind the noise of the breakfast trays being stacked, and Rita laughing with the friend you couldn't see, and Mrs. D. calling, *Up your bum*, it was quiet as new sky. I was empty. I could lift like tree and fly away. I could follow the smoke up toward the ceiling and sneak out through the cracks in the windows.

I didn't want my breakfast. I was hot and cold all over. Vomit waited in the hot corridor of my throat. My bones shook. Norma ate her breakfast and watched me. She said, "The blue shoes will come for you. He'll take you to the washing room."

"Why?"

"So he can do what he wants to you. I want to stop him."

"What will he do?"

"Whatever he wants."

"What?"

"Hurt you."

"How?"

"Any way he wants."

"When?"

"I don't know when. Soon. Will you be all right?"

The blade of a small knife caught in my throat when I swallowed. I had no answer.

Norma's eyes were wide. "He'll be here soon."

I sent a picture down the rope to Norma. It was me and Norma inside a white egg. The shell was one you couldn't break.

I was sleeping when a hand on my shoulder woke me. "Get up," said the blue shoes. "Get up now." The blade twisted tight in my throat. There was vomit waiting. The Lord held my head very tight between his finger and thumb. He was squeezing. The blue shoes whispered, "Move it!" and shook me. I got up. "Follow me." Norma was sitting up in her bed as we walked past.

Blue shoes took me to the washing room. "Get on the floor," he said.

"What for?" I asked him. How do you clean a floor when you are lying on it?

"Get on the floor." He pushed me down very hard, then undid his belt and pulled down his trousers. "I'm putting you to use," he said. His smile had a thorn. He pulled my pants down and smacked my nose. I saw the bump in his undertrousers.

A tickle started in my middle. Blue shoes had hard arms; he was big, but I was bigger. He pulled my legs apart. He pinched my skin very hard. My skin burned. I put my hands on the face of the blue shoes as he came close. "Crazy slut!" His words caught in the cracks between my fingers, just like mine used to, with Boot's hand over my mouth. My hands on his face slippery as oil, his hair fell off like a rat; it made me laugh and I pulled him onto me. He tried to take my hands away from his face. He tried to smack my nose again but I put one hand over his mouth and his eyes, then took his ear and pinched. I pulled him closer. The blue shoes wriggled. He didn't know whether to be happy or scared. My legs spread one apart from the other, far from each other yet wanting to go farther. The middle of me was wet as the sink, you can put your tree in me Mr. blue shoes and *in!* he went *push push!*

His mouth was wider and wetter than Boot's mouth. His hands were spades that dug up the dirt of me; they made me a hole for climbing in, filling me up with mud. Blue shoes' tree moved in me. My head fell off my neck—hit the floor, *bump!* My hands fell off my arms, feet fell off my legs, all rolled in pieces around me. Blue shoes and me rocked like Moses in the reeds, like the baby cradle, like Boot on Sack when I watched through the crack. Then the baby cradle broke, I tasted my Boot and my Sack fresh in my mouth, and then I smacked the blue shoes hard in his eye and one more time in his teeth.

He tried to get up. I pulled him back. My mouth was wet and full with tears and hard sick. I looked right into the scared eye of the blue shoes, and I spat. The blue shoes stood up faster than the little fast mouse needing his hole in the wall. He wiped his eye. He pulled up his trousers. The snake on his arm slithered off and disappeared under the washing room door. The blue shoes shook like green jelly in a bowl. "We have to get back." I followed him to the dormitory. Norma was sitting up in bed with a white face and a wide eye. I sent a picture of me on a boat. The boat was rocking on the stormy ocean. I sailed back to where Norma waited on the shore. After that Norma lay down and I got in my bed and went to sleep.

The blue shoes didn't look at me the next day. Not in the smoking room or the Airing Court or the dining room. Blue shoes was mouse pretending he had a hole to hide in, he was Boot pretending the night visit never was, looking anywhere but in my eyes.

Hot water dripped from under my hair, down my face; hot water in my eyes stopped me seeing. Hot water down my back, under my arms, down my legs. I shook, I couldn't stand. Jesus played his drum in my head. I vomited on my knees in the Airing Court. I vomited in the washing room while a blue shoes washed me. I vomited while Nurse Clegg and a blue shoes took me to the sick room and locked me in. I vomited green and then I vomited nothing but gray air and heat. Needles went into my bone and the world turned to moving cloud. I was tied down inside the cloud with straps.

You breathed hard with your mouth wide open—it was a *laugh* you were doing! It was the devil's language you spoke. This was the loudest laugh you ever made; your mouth was the hole the laugh came through but it was your body that made this laugh. This laugh made your body go *long short long short*, this laugh hurt you but could you stop it? *No!* This laugh did what it wanted, this laugh was bigger than you. It was bigger than the green-sheeted bed you lay on, bigger than the sick room Nurse Clegg locked you in, bigger than One Cott Road and the dark street. This laugh came at the end of the world; this was the last laugh.

The song was loud in your head with words that played over and over, lovely words, loud like bells. *"I danced on the Sabbath when I cured the lame / The holy people said it was a shame / They whipped and they stripped and they hung me high / And they left me there on a cross to die."* Your feet felt warm. This warmth moved up from your feet into your legs and then into your middle. The middle of you grew hotter *hotter*, heat spread through you—Hester, you were a girl on fire! It was you in the red wood stove, you burning up, flame and fire coming from your fingers and toes and tongue as you screamed, *More wood more wood!* It was your turn to burn, like tree, axe, and spoon. God the Bird and Jesus watched. They waited to see if you would go to them where they waited in eternity.

From somewhere behind your song you heard cool voices. The voices moved you to another room, they wrapped you in green-water sheets, but you did not cool *no no*. You kept burning! You were too hot for them. The cool voices tried to touch you and you left little red spiders on their arms and faces. You burned a long time. *Burn burn burn* until the world turned to ash.

God the Bird came down; he landed on the branch of a burnt black tree. He held out his wing. Just as I was about to climb on he opened his beak and said, "Remember the promise you made."

My promise floated in front of me in the shape of a kite made of a golden dress. It flew in circles through the air, turning itself into a question, then back to a kite again. I held on to the string and I was lifted over the world where I saw all the people's faces turned up to see me flying over. As I floated, carried by the promise, I saw Norma's face and it had a tear and it had hope. Hope is what Jesus gave to the corrupted.

I was out of the sickbed and back in the morning room. Some of my pile of sin was left behind in the sickbed, and some in the hands of the white dress who put needles in me and said, *You'll live.* My green suit hung off me like I was an empty coat in the cupboard. I sat with my back against the wall. Norma came over to me. She was crying. "What happened to you? Where did you go?" I had no strength in my bones for moving. I couldn't lift a fag for smoking. The wall held me up. Norma hit me on the chest. "Where did you go? You said you wouldn't go!"

A blues shoes came over and put Norma back against the wall. "Easy, Norma. She's been sick."

Norma was breathing hard, her body filling up and emptying fast. "Did you get sick?" she asked me. "Did you? Is that what happened?"

I looked over Norma's head for the black birds. There were none. "I made a promise," I told Norma, and then I gave her my biggest smile. Norma's body slowly emptied, then she leaned back against the wall and took my hand.

We were walking in the Airing Court when Norma stopped me. "I spoke to my brother last night, Hester. He asked me to come and live with him again. He wants to take care of me." We leaned against the wire and looked out at the green world beyond. The wire broke the green world into pieces. "I think I could do it now, Hester. The devil's not coming back because of you. He's gone." She put her fingers into the holes and pulled. "I mean if I wanted to, I could do it."

There was a long quiet. I closed my eyes and I saw the happy face of Norma looking at a river of fast-running water without the walls of Renton telling it when to stop. I took a long breath of air deep inside me. "You can go, Norma," I said.

She turned to me. "But I'd never leave you. You know that. I'd find a way for you to come too, or I wouldn't go."

"Norma, you can go."

Norma started to cry. "But I'd find a way for you to come too. That's what I'd do."

"You can go and live with your brother near the river. The devil's gone now, he's not coming back."

"But—"

I took her hand, "I will be all right—you can go."

"I love you, Hester."

I lay in bed that night, lifted my arms from the covers, and drew pictures in the air of Norma's brother driving in circles over the roof of Renton in his white chariot. Wings grew from the sides, just under the windows. Pebblinghaus ran out onto the gravel path, looked up, and pointed at Harrison. All the blue shoes ran out and stood beside Pebblinghaus. Teacups sat on their heads. Nurse Clegg poured pink into the teacups. The blue shoes bent over and drank from each other's cups and then they fell asleep where they stood as Norma's brother drove right through the front door of Renton. Norma climbed into the chariot and waved to me as she flew away with her brother, lights shining from the wheels.

"Good-bye, Norma," I said to the picture hanging in the darkness over my head. In my throat there was stone.

We sat in the game room. Ladies looked at the box of tricks. Soldiers locked in the box ran toward a ball. Some fell over and that's when ladies laughed. Norma laughed too; her face was a flower. There was no laugh in me. In the box of tricks was a world without Norma.

. . .

Nurse Clegg came to us in the Airing Court. "Your brother is here for you, Norma." Norma took hold of me and held me tight; I could feel her heart beat against my chest through her thin shirt. It was the living Norma. She held me and then she let me go. I watched her follow Nurse Clegg back inside.

I sat down on the hard ground. I leaned my head back against the wire and closed my eyes. I looked for patterns behind my lids but there was nothing, not light or dark—only emptiness, the same emptiness that was in the fish's head when you pulled out the eye. There was no bottom to it. I don't know how long I sat—was it one hour, one day, or eighteen years? A foot touched mine.

"Up you get, time to go back inside." Nurse Clegg frowned down at me.

I was sitting in front of the box of tricks in the game room. "Will you come with me? I spoke to Harrison. We can buy you out of here. I will take care of you. You've got to come or I'm not going." It was Norma.

I started to cry. It was the loud sound of life. Norma held me tight. "I told you I'd find a way, Hester. Harrison's going to offer Pebblinghaus the money from when he sold my mother's house so that you can come with us. He said nothing will stand between Pebblinghaus and a bucket of money, not even you."

• • •

I lay in my bed and watched my paintings fly around the dormitory, their paper wings rustling and flapping. When they stopped still they turned themselves into the walls of a paper house for Norma, Harrison, and me.

We were in the front room at Renton. Norma's brother was coming soon. Norma had a suitcase but I had nothing. I was wearing the dress that I wore when I first came to Renton. It was too big for me now; I floated small inside it. Norma looked scared; she held on to me as though I would float away if she didn't.

We sat on two hard-backed chairs. Pebblinghaus was behind the desk but she never looked at us. She was busy watering the garden with the bucket of money that Harrison was going to give her. The clock above the desk ticked loudly as the hands turned around. Neither of us moved.

A man came through the door. Norma ran to him. "Harrison!" She jumped on him. He nearly fell backward. He put her down. "This is Harrison," said Norma. Harrison's face was hiding in hair. Some of the hair was gray, some of it was red, and some of it was brown. He smiled. He had a gap too, on the other side from Norma. His eyes were the color of leaves in the autumn.

Pebblinghaus said, "Good-bye, Norma," from behind a desk. She pretended she couldn't see me but she didn't stop me leaving.

"Come on, Hester," said Norma. I didn't know where I was going. But wherever I was going it was with Norma. I made a promise. I followed Norma and Harrison to the chariot. This time it was a brown one with a tray-box on the back.

The three of us sat in the front seat. When Harrison got in the chariot he put a hat with a lot of holes in it on his head and pulled the sleeves of his shirt up. On his arms there were drawings of an anchor and a boat but the boat wasn't inside a bottle. It was sailing on the sea and a lady with a fish tail was jumping out of the sea beside it. It was Lot's wife; she had gone to the deepest bottom where it was all salty and she had come up half made of fish and she could swim and wave. Harrison saw me looking. "That's Lillian. My good luck girl. It looks like she's worked her magic—Norma's coming home. She says she wouldn't be coming home if it wasn't for you. I figure I owe you as well as her."

"And now we got no money," said Norma, smiling her gap. She had an arm through her brother's. Lillian the good luck girl sat close to the streets cut into Norma's arm.

"But we got a home," said Harrison.

We were on the road away from Renton. The wind blew in through the open window. Tall trees on the sides waved their silver leaves. The sun was shining on us from her big home. We didn't speak but we sent pictures along the ropes to each other. Harrison sent one to me of him and Norma when they were little. They were eating cobs of corn and jumping through water. I sent one to Norma, of me and Mary standing at the edge of the puddle, and Norma sent one to me and Harrison of her by herself at Renton looking at the streets across her arms and not knowing what would happen next. I turned back and looked to see if I could see myself holding on to the wire in the Airing Court of Renton, but Renton was too far behind.

We drove in the chariot until the day turned to night. The sun sank into a bed of bright orange. There were black lines mixed in, the way black paint cuts through a red painting. Norma slept with her head on my shoulder, then on Harrison's shoulder, then back to mine. Harrison stopped at a place as light as Renton, full of other chariots. He said, "You girls can go to the bathroom, and I'll get something for us to eat." I followed Norma to the toilets. There were no blue shoes. I asked Norma, I said, "Where are the blue shoes?" She said, "Those days are over." Harrison came back to the car with pink sweets and biscuits with chocolate and a pie. We ate them as he drove. The sweetness filled me. I was made of light. Eternity was inside me and it had no walls, floors, or ceiling. It was dark as night and light as the stars and it was full of pencils.

In the morning, when the sun came out again, we were in the forest that Norma had told me about in the Renton washing room. Norma stretched and yawned. "Are we there yet?" she asked.

Harrison said, "You've been asking that since you were five."

"Well, are we?" Norma rubbed her eyes.

"Just at the end of this track."

The chariot bounced up and down as we drove. The road was made of small rocks and dirt and it got thinner as we went along. Branches from the trees on the side pushed at the windows. There was a bird with feathers that curled up. The bird whistled. Harrison said, "That's my friend, Douglas. He's a lyrebird. If I could catch him I could play a tune on his tail."

Harrison stopped the chariot in front of a wooden house. It was the same color as the trees all around it. A dog came out. "This is Harvey," said Harrison. "It's only been me, Douglas, and Harvey for a long time. We're not used to female company. You'll have to teach us the ropes." He showed his tooth gap to us again when he smiled and then Norma bent down and Harvey licked her face.

Harrison took us inside. A long wooden table stood in the middle of the room. It had lots of things on it: oranges, candles, teacups, lemons, ashtrays, and scattered pencils with paper. Not one chair around the table was the same as another. The window on the wall above one end of the table was a picture made of colored glass—Christ was forgiving the hunter in blue and purple. The hunter was on his knee with the spear down low. There were spiderwebs in the corners of the room and dust on the ledges. The sun showed it floating. Harvey jumped up and sat on a big brown chair between a hat and a book. Paintings of creeks, setting suns, and horses hung on the walls. Somebody did them with pencils.

Harrison filled a kettle with water. "I built it myself, so there's none of the mod cons. But I made up a couple of beds for you. You can figure out how you want to set things up."

"You've done so much, Harrison. It looks great. It's big enough." Norma looked around. She picked a plate up from the table, then put it down. Then she picked up a dirty pot, put that down, and started to cry. I cried too and then so did Harrison. Harrison looked away and blew his nose on a handkerchief. Norma didn't look away and neither did I. Harrison gave her a cuddle. "It's over now. *I'll* look after *you* this time. I can take care of everything."

Norma stepped back. "Come with me, Hester." She saw me looking at the pencils. "You can use those as much as you want later, can't she, Harrison? Come on, come with me."

I followed Norma out of the house that Harrison built. At the bottom of the garden was a rusted gate made of lace with no fence on either side. Norma laughed as she opened the gate, and we passed through into a forest. Trees came close, red birds flew down, the ground was moving with beetles, worms, flies. The wind sang along with the birds. *Alleluia, dance for joy.* Somebody played a tune on Douglas's blue tail. It was the forbidden outside.

Norma walked along the track in front of me. I followed her bare feet over dirt and fallen leaves. The sun was hot on my shoulders. I looked up to the empty, blue sky. It never ended and I was part of it.

Norma and me stepped out of the edge of the forest and there was the river. It was made of wild running water and white bubbles. The river laughed as it rushed, tickled by the green ropy branches that hung on the sides and touched its bubbling surface.

Norma and me pulled off our clothes. Our bodies were shining. We stepped into the water. It was cold on my legs and then it was cold on my stomach. The pebbles were smooth under my feet. Norma went under like John the Baptist. I went under too. Water rushed over my head. I opened my eyes and Harrison's good luck girl swam toward me. She touched my hair. I came up into the warm light. Norma flipped like a fish. "I love you, Hester!"

We lay on the bank of the river, the earth gritty and cool on our backs and legs. The sun dried our skin. A beetle with green and pink spirals in its wing crawled across my hills to the other side, then flew into the reeds. We sat up, trailing our toes in the water. Norma picked up my shirt and put it across my shoulders. She lit two cigarettes. The fire sticks crackled as we sucked back the smoke. When we let it out, the smoke billowed around our faces then lifted, drifting over us, slowly curling up and around the trees, over the house that Harrison built, over the river, over the forest, then higher, into the light of the sun, and beyond, into eternity.

But the day of the Lord will come as a thief in the night.

2 Peter 3:10

Special thanks to:

Jane Palfreyman, Rob Ryan (Clinical Nurse Consultant, North Western Mental Health), Sue Walsh, Richard Walsh, Gail Jones, Laura Harris, Bianca Martino, Michelle Madden, Kim Kane, Sandy Webster, staff and students at RMIT (Professional Writing and Editing), Brigid Arnott, Joanna Wilkinson and Marc McBride.